Theodore Frelinghuysen Wolfe

Literary shrines

The haunts of some famous American authors

Theodore Frelinghuysen Wolfe

Literary shrines
The haunts of some famous American authors

ISBN/EAN: 9783337281410

Printed in Europe, USA, Canada, Australia, Japan

Cover: Foto ©Andreas Hilbeck / pixelio.de

More available books at **www.hansebooks.com**

LITERARY SHRINES

THE HAUNTS OF SOME FAMOUS AMERICAN AUTHORS

BY THEODORE F. WOLFE
M.D. Ph.D.

AUTHOR OF A LITERARY PILGRIMAGE ETC.

J. B. LIPPINCOTT COMPANY
PHILADELPHIA. MDCCCXCV

TO

MY WIFE,

MY SYMPATHETIC AND APPRECIATIVE
COMPANION IN PILGRIMAGES
TO MANY

LITERARY SHRINES

IN THE NEW WORLD AND THE OLD,

THIS VOLUME

IS AFFECTIONATELY INSCRIBED.

PREFACE

FOR some years it has been the delightful privilege of the writer of the present volume to ramble and sojourn in the scenes amid which his best-beloved authors erst lived and wrote. He has made repeated pilgrimages to most of the shrines herein described, and has been, at one time or another, favored by intercourse and correspondence with many of the authors adverted to or with their surviving friends and neighbors. In the ensuing pages he has endeavored to portray these shrines in pen-pictures which, it is hoped, may be interesting to those who are unable to visit them and helpful and companionable for those who can and will. If certain prominent American authors receive little more than mention in these pages, it is mainly because so few objects and places associated with their lives and writings can now be indisputably identified: in some instances the writer has expended more time upon fruitless quests for shrines which proved to be non-existent or of doubtful genuineness than upon others which are themes for the chapters of this booklet.

T. F. W.

CONTENTS

THE CONCORD PILGRIMAGE

9

Contents

IN AND OUT OF LITERARY BOSTON

IN BOSTON

OUT OF BOSTON

Contents

Contents

IN BERKSHIRE WITH HAWTHORNE

A DAY WITH THE GOOD GRAY POET

ILLUSTRATIONS

13

THE CONCORD PILGRIMAGE

I

A VILLAGE OF LITERARY SHRINES

Abodes of Thoreau — The Alcotts — Channing — Sanborn — Hudson — Hoar — Wheildon — Bartlett — The Historic Common — Cemetery — Church.

IF to trace the footsteps of genius and to linger and muse in the sometime haunts of the authors we read and love, serve to bring us nearer their personality, to place us *en rapport* with their aspirations, and thus to incite our own spiritual development and broaden and exalt our moral nature, then the Concord pilgrimage should be one of the most fruitful and beneficent of human experiences. Familiarity with the physical stand-point of our authors, with the scenes amid which they lived and wrote, and with the objects which suggested the imagery of their poems, the settings of their tales, and which gave tone and color to their work, will not only bring us into closer sympathy with the writers, but will help us to a better understanding of the writings.

A plain, straggling village, set in a low country amid a landscape devoid of any striking beauty or grandeur, Concord yet attracts more pilgrims than any other place of equal size upon the continent, not because it holds an historic battle-field, but because it has been the dwelling-place of some of the brightest and best in American letters, who have here written their books and warred against creeds, forms, and intellectual servitude. It is another Stratford, another Mecca, to which come reverent pilgrims from the Old World and the New to worship at its shrines and to wander through the scenes hallowed by the memories of its illustrious *littérateurs*, seers, and evangels.. To the literary prowler it is all sacred ground,—its streets, its environing hills, forests, lakes, and streams have alike been blessed by the loving presence of genius, have alike been the theatres and the inspirations of noble literary achievement.

Our way lies by historic Lexington, and thence, through a pleasant country and by the road so fateful to the British soldiery, we approach Concord. It is a placid, almost somnolent village of villas, abounding with delightful lawns and gardens, with great elms shading its old-fashioned thoroughfares and drooping their pliant boughs above its comfortable homes.

Elizabeth Hoar has said, "Concord is Thoreau's monument, adorned with inscriptions by his hand;" of the circle of brilliant souls who have given the town its world-wide fame, he alone was native here; he has left his imprint upon the place, and we meet some reminder of him at every turn. By the historic village Common is the quondam home of his grandfather, where his father was reared, and where the "New England Essene" himself lived some time with the unmarried aunt who made the ample homespun suit he wore at Walden. The house of his maternal grandmother, where Henry David Thoreau was born, stood a little way out on a by-road to Lexington, and a daughter of this home—Thoreau's winsome aunt Louisa Dunbar—was ineffectually wooed by the famous Daniel Webster. At the age of eight months the infant Thoreau was removed to the village, in which nearly the whole of his life was passed. Believing that Concord, with its sylvan environment, was a microcosm " by the study of which the whole world could be comprehended," this wildest of civilized men seldom strayed beyond its familiar precincts. Alcott declared that Thoreau thought he dwelt in the centre of the universe, and seriously contemplated annexing the rest of the planet to Concord.

On the south side of the elm-shaded Main street of the village we find a pleasant and comfortable, old-fashioned wooden dwelling,—the home which, in his later years, the philosopher, poet, and mystic shared with his mother and sisters. About it are great trees which Thoreau planted; a stairway and some of the partition walls of the house are said to have been erected by him. In the second story of an extension at the back of the main edifice, some of the family worked at their father's trade of pencil-making. In the large room at the right of the entrance, afterward the sitting-room of the Alcotts, some of Thoreau's later writing was done, and here, one May morning of 1862, he breathed out a life all too brief and doubtless abbreviated by the storms and drenchings endured in his pan-theistic pursuits. In this house Thoreau's " spir-itual brother," John Brown of Osawatomie, was a welcome guest, and more than one wretched fugitive from slavery found shelter and protec-tion. From his village home Thoreau made, with the poet Ellery Channing, the journey described in his " Yankee in Canada," and sev-eral shorter " Excursions,"—shared with Ed-ward Hoar, Channing, and others,—which he has detailed in the delightful manner which gives him a distinct position in American literature.

After the removal of Sophia, the last of Thoreau's family, his friend Frank B. Sanborn

occupied the Thoreau house for some years, and then it became the home of the Alcott family. Here Mrs. Alcott, the "Marmee" of "Little Women," died; here Bronson Alcott was stricken with the fatal paralysis; here commenced the malady which contributed to the death of his illustrious daughter Louisa; here lived "Meg," the mother of the "Little Men" and widow of "John Brooke" of the Alcott books; and here now lives her son, while his brother, "Demi-John," dwells just around the corner in the next street. In the room at the left of the hall, fitted up for her study and workshop, Louisa Alcott wrote some of the tales which the world will not forget. An added apartment at the right of the sitting-room was long the sick-room of the Orphic philosopher and the scene of Louisa's tender care. Here the writer saw them both for the last time: Alcott helpless upon his couch, his bright intelligence dulled by a veil of darkness; the daughter at his bedside, sedulous of his comfort, devoted, hopeful, helpful to the end. A cherished memento of that interview is a photograph of the Thoreau-Alcott mansion, made by one of the "Little Men," and presented to the writer, with her latest book, by "Jo" herself. The front fence has since been removed, and the illustration shows the present view.

The Concord Pilgrimage

In Thoreau's time, a modest dwelling, with a low roof sloping to the rear,—now removed to the other side of the street,—stood directly opposite his home, and was for some time the abode of his friend and earliest biographer, the sweet poet William Ellery Channing. Thoreau thought Channing one of the few who understood "the art of taking walks," and the two were almost constant companions in saunterings through the countryside, or in idyllic excursions upon the river in the boat which Thoreau kept moored to a riverside willow at the foot of Channing's garden. The beneficent influence of their comradeship is apparent in the work of both these recluse writers, and many of the most charming of Channing's stanzas are either inspired by or are poetic portrayals of the scenes he saw with Thoreau,—the " Rudolpho" and the "Idolon" of his verse. Thoreau's last earthly "Excursion" was with this friend to Monadnoc, where they encamped some days in 1860. To this home of Channing came, in 1855, Sanborn, who was welcomed to Concord by all the literary galaxy, and quickly became a familiar associate of each particular star. To go swimming together seems to have been, among these earnest and exalted thinkers, the highest evidence of mutual esteem, and so favored was Sanborn that he is able to record, " I have swum with Alcott in Thoreau's Cove, with Thoreau in the Assabet, with Channing in every water of Concord."

In this home Sanborn entertained John Brown on the eve of his Virginia venture ; here escaping slaves found refuge ; here fugitives from the Harper's Ferry fight were concealed; here Sanborn was arrested for supposed complicity in Brown's abortive schemes, and was forcibly rescued by his indignant neighbors. This modest dwelling gave place to the later residence of Frederic Hudson, the historian of journalism, who here produced many of his contributions to literature. Professor Folsom, of " Translations of the Four Gospels," and the popular authoress Mrs. Austin have also lived in this neighborhood.

For some years Sanborn had a famous select school on a street back of Thoreau's house, not far from the recent hermit-home of his friend Channing, at whose request Hawthorne sent some of his children to this school, in which Emerson's daughter—the present Mrs. Forbes— was a beloved pupil, and where, also, the daughters of John Brown were for some time placed.

A few rods westward from his former dwelling we find Sanborn in a tasteful modern villa,—

spending life's early autumn among his books. He abounds with memories of his friends of the by-gone time, and his reminiscences and biographies of some of them have largely employed his pen in his pleasant study here.

Some time ago the sweet singer Channing suffered in his hermitage a severe illness, which prompted his appreciative friend Sanborn to take him into his own home; so we find two surviving witnesses or participants in the moral, intellectual, and political renaissance dwelling under the same roof. In the kindly atmosphere of this home, the shy poet—who in his age is more recluse than ever, and scarce known to his neighbors—so far regained physical vigor that he has resumed his frequent visits to the Boston library, long time a favorite haunt of his. The world refused to listen to this exquisite singer, and now "his songs have ceased." He has been celebrated by Emerson in the "Dial," by Thoreau in his "Week," by Hawthorne in "Mosses" and "Note-Books," by the generous and sympathetic Sanborn in many ways and places; but even such poems as "Earth-Spirit," "Poet's Hope," and "Reverence" found few readers,—the dainty little volumes fewer purchasers.

Below the Thoreau-Alcott house on the village street was a prior home of Thoreau, from which he made, with his brother, the voyage described in his "Week on the Concord and Merrimac Rivers," and from which, in superb disdain of "civilization" and social convention-alities, he went to the two years' hermitage of "Walden."

Nearly opposite the earlier residence of the stoic is the home of the Hoars, where lived Thoreau's comrade Edward Hoar, and Edward's sister,—styled "Elizabeth the Wise" by Emerson, of whom she was the especial friend and favorite, having been the *fiancée* of his brother Charles, who died in early manhood. The adjacent spacious mansion was long the home of Wheildon, the historian, essayist, and pamphleteer. Nearer the village Common lived John A. Stone, dramatist of "The Ancient Briton" and of the "Metamora" in which Forrest won his first fame. In this part of the village the eminent correspondent "Warrington," author of "Manual of Parliamentary Law," was born and reared; and in Lowell Street, not far away, lives the gifted George B. Bartlett, of the "Carnival of Authors,"—poet, scenic artist, and local historian.

In the public library we find copies of the printed works of the many Concord authors, and portraits or busts of most of the writers.

The Concord Pilgrimage

Among the treasures of the institution are priceless manuscripts of Curtis, Motley, Lowell, Holmes, Emerson, Hawthorne, Thoreau, and others.

Among the thickly-strewn graves on the hillside above the Common repose the ashes of Emerson's ancestors; about them lie the forefathers of the settlement,—some of them asleep here for two centuries, reckless alike of the resistance to British oppression and of the later struggle for freedom of thought which their townsmen have waged. A tree on the Common is pointed out as that beneath which Emerson made an address at the dedication of the soldiers' monument, and Bartlett records the tradition that the grandfather of the Concord sage stood on the same spot a hundred years before to harangue the "embattled farmers" on the morning of the Concord fight.

Near by is the ancient church where Emerson's ancestors preached, and within whose framework the Provincial Congress met. Of the religious services here Emerson was always a supporter, often an attendant; here he sometimes preached in early manhood; here his children were christened by the elder Channing, —"the first minister he had known who was as good as they;" here Emerson's daughter is a devout worshipper.

A Village of Literary Shrines

The comparatively few of the transcendental company who prayed within a pew came to this temple, but here all were brought at last for funeral rites: here lay Thoreau among his thronging townsmen while Emerson and Bronson Alcott made their touching eulogies and Ellery Channing read a dirge in a voice almost hushed with emotion; here James Freeman Clarke, who had married Hawthorne twenty-two years before, preached his funeral sermon above the lifeless body which bore upon its breast the unfinished " Dolliver Romance;" before the pulpit here lay the coffined Emerson,— " his eyes forever closed, his voice forever still," —while a vast concourse looked upon him for the last time, and his neighbor Judge Hoar pronounced one of the most impressive panegyrics that ever fell from human lips, and the devoted Alcott read a sonnet.

II

THE OLD MANSE

NORTHWARD from the village Common, a delightful stroll along a shaded highway, less secluded now than when Hawthorne "daily trudged" upon it to the post-office or trundled the carriage of "baby Una," brings us to the famous "Old Manse" about which he culled his "Mosses."

This antique mansion was first tenanted by Ralph Waldo Emerson's grandsire, and next by Dr. Ezra Ripley, who married the previous occupant's widow and became guardian of her children,—born under its roof,—of whom Emerson's father was one. When his father died Emerson found a secondary home here with Dr. Ripley. The Manse was again the abode of Emerson and his mother in 1834–35, when he here wrote his first volume. In 1842, the year following the demise of the good Dr. Ripley, the Manse was profaned by its first lay occupant, Nathaniel Hawthorne. He brought here his bride, lovely Sophia Peabody (who, with the gifted Elizabeth and Mrs. Horace Mann, formed a famous triune sisterhood), and for four years lived here the ideal life of which his "Note-Books" and "Mosses" give us such delicious glimpses. Hawthorne's landlord, Samuel Ripley, was related to the George Ripley with whom Hawthorne had recently been associated at Brook Farm. He was uncle of Emerson, and preached his ordination sermon; was himself reared in the old Manse, and succeeded Hawthorne as resident there. His widow, born Sarah Bradford, and celebrated as "the most learned woman ever seen in New England," the close friend of Emerson and of the brilliant Concord company, survived here until 1876. She made a valuable collection of lichens, and sometimes trained young men for Harvard University. Conway records that a *savant* called here one day and found her hearing at once the lesson of one student in Sophocles and that of another in Differential Calculus, while rocking her grandchild's cradle with one foot and shelling peas for dinner. The place is now owned by her daughters, who reside in Cambridge, and is rented in summer.

It is little changed since the time Emerson's ancestor hurried thence to the gathering of his parishioners by his church-door before the Concord battle,—still less changed since the halcyon days when the great wizard of romance dwelt—the "most unknown of authors"—within its shades. It is still the unpretentious Eden, "the El Dorado for dreamers," which so completely won the heart of the sensitive Hawthorne.

The picturesque old mansion stands amid greensward and foliage, its ample grounds divided from the highway by a low wall. The gate-way is flanked by tall posts of rough-hewn stone, whence a grass-grown avenue, bordered by a colonnade of overarching trees, leads to the house. Within the scattered sunshine and shade of the avenue, a row of stone slabs sunken in the turf like gravestones paves the path paced by Ripley, Emerson, and Hawthorne as they pondered and planned their compositions. Of the trees aligned upon either side, some, gray-lichened and broken, are survivors of Hawthorne's time; others are set to replace fallen patriarchs and keep the stately lines complete. At the right of the broad *allée* and extending away to the battle-ground is the field, waving now with lush grass, where Hawthorne and Thoreau found the flint arrow-heads and other relics of an aboriginal village. Upon the space which skirts the other side of the avenue, Hawthorne had the garden which engaged so much of his

time and thought, and where he produced for
us abundant crops of something better than his
vegetables. Here his Brook-Farm experience
was useful. Passing neighbors would often see
the darkly-clad figure of the recluse hoeing in
this "patch," or, as often, standing motionless,
gazing upon the ground so fixedly and so long
—sometimes for hours together—that they
thought him daft. Of the delights of summer
mornings spent here with his peas, potatoes,
and squashes, he gives us many glimpses in his
record of that happy time; but the "Note-
Books" show us, alas! that this simple pleasure
was not without alloy, for, although his "garden flourished like Eden," there are hints of
"weeds," next "more weeds," then a "fero-
cious banditti of weeds" with which "the
other Adam" could never have contended.
But a greater woe came with the foes who
menaced his artistic squashes,—"the uncon-
scionable squash-bugs," "those infernal squash-
bugs," against which he must "carry on con-
tinual war." For the moments that we contemplate the scene of his entomic warfare, the
greater battle-field, a few rods away, seems
hardly more impressive. Few of the trees
which in Hawthorne's time stood nearest the
house remain; the producers of the peaches

and "thumping pears" have gone the way of all trees. So has Dr. Ripley's famous willow —celebrated in Emerson's and Channing's exquisite verse and in Hawthorne's matchless prose —which veiled the western face of the mansion and through which Hawthorne's study-windows peeped out upon orchard, river, and mead. In the orchard that has borne such luscious fruit of fancy, some of the contorted and moss-grown trees, whose branches—"like withered hands and arms"—hold out the sweet blossoms on this June day, are the same that Hawthorne pictures among his "Mosses," and beneath which he lay in summer reverie. Few vines now clamber upon the house-walls, lilacs still grow beneath the old study-window, and a tall mass of their foliage screens a corner of the venerable edifice, which time has toned into perfect harmony with its picturesque environment. It is a great, square, wooden structure of two stories, with added attic rooms beneath an overwhelming gambrel roof, which is the conspicuous feature of the edifice and contributes to its antique form. The heavy roof settles down close upon the small, multipaned windows. From above the door little convex glasses, like a row of eyes, look out upon the visitor as he applies for admission.

The Old Manse

A spacious central hall, rich in antique panelling and sombre with grave tints, extends through the house. From its dusk and coolness we look out upon the bright summer day through its open doors; through one we see the "hill of the Emersons" beyond the highway, the other frames a pleasing picture of orchard and sward with glimpses of the river shining through its bordering shrubbery. The quaint apartments are darkly wainscoted and low-ceiled, with massive beams crossing overhead. Some of these rooms Hawthorne has shown us. The one at the left, which the novelist believed to have been the sleeping-room of Dr. Ripley, was the parlor of the Hawthornes, and — decked with a gladsome carpet, pictures, and flowers daily gathered from the river-bank — Hawthorne averred it was " one of the prettiest and pleasantest rooms in the whole world." To this room then came the sage Emerson "with a sunbeam in his face;" the " cast-iron man" Thoreau, " long-nosed, queer-mouthed, ugly as sin," but with whom to talk " is like hearing the wind among the boughs of a forest tree ;" Ellery Channing, with his wife and her illustrious sister, Margaret Fuller; the gifted George William Curtis, then tilling a farm not far from the Manse, long before he lounged in an " Easy Chair;" genial Bradford, relative of Ripley, and associate and firm friend of Hawthorne; Horatio Bridge, of the " African Cruiser" and of the recent Hawthorne " Recollections;" the critic George Hilliard, at whose house Hawthorne was married; " Prince" Lowell, the large-hearted; Franklin Pierce, Hawthorne's life-long friend. Concerning the discussion of things physical and metaphysical, to which these old walls then listened, the host gives us little hint. Sometimes the guests were " feasted on nectar and ambrosia" by the new Adam and Eve; sometimes they " listened to the music of the spheres which, for private convenience, is packed into a musicbox,"—left here by Thoreau when he went to teach in the family of Emerson's brother; once here before this wide fireplace they sat late and told ghost stories,—doubtless suggested by the clerical phantom whose sighs they used to hear in yonder dusky corner, and whose rustling gown sometimes almost touched the company as he moved about among them. In this room Dr. Ripley penned, besides his " History of the Concord Fight" and " Treatise on Education," three thousand of his protracted homilies,—a fact upon which Hawthorne found it " awful to reflect,"—and here in our day the

The Old Manse

gifted George B. Bartlett wrote some part of his Concord sketches, etc. Here, too, and in the larger room opposite, the erudite and versatile Mrs. Samuel Ripley held her social court and received the exalted Concord conclave, with other earnest leaders of thought.

In the front chamber at the right Hawthorne's first child, the hapless Una,—named from Spenser's "Faerie Queene,"—was born. Behind this is the "ten-foot-square" apartment which was Hawthorne's study and workshop. Two windows of small, prismatic-hued panes look into the orchard, and upon one of these Hawthorne has inscribed,—

"Nath¹. Hawthorne.
This is his study, 1843."

Below this another hand has graven,—

"Inscribed by my husband at
Sunset Apr 3ᵈ 1843
In the gold light   S. A. H.
Man's accidents are God's purposes.
SOPHIA A. HAWTHORNE 1843."

From its north window, said to have been cracked by the explosions of musketry in the conflict, we see the battle-field and a reach of the placid river. This room had been the study of Emerson's grandfather; from its window his wife watched the fight between his undrilled parishioners and the British veterans. His daughter Mary—aunt of our American Plato and herself a gifted writer—used to boast " she was in arms at the battle," having been held up at this window to see the soldiery in the highway. Years later Emerson himself came into possession of this room, and here wrote his " Nature," antagonizing many of the orthodox tenets. Perhaps it was well for the moral serenity of his ancestor—to whom the transcendental movement would have seemed arrant March-madness—that he could not foresee the composition of such a volume here within the sanctity of his old study. The book was published anonymously, and Sanborn says that when inquiry was made, " Who is the author of ' Nature ?' " a Concord wit replied, " God and Waldo Emerson."

Next, the dreamy Hawthorne succeeded to the little study, and here, with the sunlight glimmering through the willow boughs, he worked in solitude upon his charming productions for three or four hours of each day. Here, besides the copious entries in his journals, he prepared most of the papers of his " Mosses," wrote many articles for the " Democratic Review" and other magazines, edited " Old Dartmoor Prisoner" and Horatio Bridge's " African Cruiser." It is noteworthy that the " Celestial Railroad," in which Hawthorne records his condemnation of the spiritual renaissance by substituting the " terrible giant Transcendentalist" (who feeds upon pilgrims bound for the Celestial City) in place of the Pope and Pagan of Bunyan's allegory, was written in the same room with Emerson's volume, which inaugurated the great transcendental movement in the Western World.

Among the recesses of the great attic of the Manse we may still see the " Saints' Chamber," with its fireplace and single window; but it is tenanted by sprouting clergymen no longer. The atmosphere of theological twilight and mustiness —acquired from generations of clerical inhabitants—which pervaded the place in Hawthorne's time has been dissipated by the larger and happier home-life of Mrs. Samuel Ripley and the blithe and brilliant company that gathered about her here. Dismayed by these beneficent influences, the ghosts have indignantly deserted the mansion: even the persistive clerical, who sighed in Hawthorne's parlor and noisily turned his sermon-leaves in the upper hall, has not disturbed the later occupants of the Manse.

One might muse and linger long about the old place which, as his " Mosses" and journals show, Hawthorne made a part of his very life. Its air of antiquity, its traditional associations, its seclusion, and all its peaceful environment were pleasing to the shy and susceptible nature of the subtle romancer, and accorded well with his introspective habit. Besides, it was "the first home he ever had," and it was shared with his "new Eve." No wonder is it that he could here declare, "I had rather be on earth than in the seventh heaven, just now."

It is saddening to remember that, from this paradise, poverty drove him forth.

III

A STORIED RIVER AND BATTLE-FIELD

Where Zenobia Drowned—Where Embattled Farmers Fought—Thoreau's Hemlocks—Haunts of Hawthorne—Channing—Thoreau—Emerson, etc.

BEHIND Hawthorne's "Old Manse"—its course so tortuous that Thoreau suggested for Concord's escutcheon "a field verdant with the river circling nine times round," so noiseless that he likened it to the "moccasined tread" of an Indian, so sluggish that Hawthorne had dwelt some weeks beside it before he determined which way its current lies—flows the Concord, "river of peace." This placid stream is the aboriginal "Musketaquid" of Emerson's poem, —sung of Thoreau, Channing, and many another bard, beloved of Hawthorne and pictured in rapturous phrase in his "Note-Books" and "Mosses from an Old Manse." It was the delightful haunt of Hawthorne's leisure, the scene of the occurrence which inspired the most thrilling and high-wrought chapter of his romance.

A grassy path, shaded by orchard trees, leads from the west door of the Manse to the river's margin at the place where Hawthorne kept his boat under the willows. The boat had before been the property of Thoreau, built by his hands and used by him on the famous voyage described in his " Week on the Concord and Merrimac Rivers." Hawthorne named the craft " Pond-Lily," because it brought so many cargoes of that beautiful flower to decorate his home. In it, alone or accompanied by Thoreau or Ellery Channing, he made the many delightful excursions he has described. Embarking on the slumberous stream, we follow the course of Hawthorne's boat to many a scene made familiar by that dreamful romancer and by the poets and philosophers of Concord. First to the place, below the bridge of the battle, where one dark night Hawthorne and Channing assisted in recovering from the water the ghastly body of the girl-suicide, an incident which made a profoundly horrible impression upon the sensitive novelist, and which he employed as the thrilling termination of the tale of Zenobia in " The Blithedale Romance,"—portraying it with a tragic power which has never been surpassed. Thence we paddle up the placid stream, as it slumbers along its winding course between the meadows, kisses the tangled grasses and wild flowers that fringe its margins, bathes the roots and boughs of the elders and dwarf willows which overhang its surface as if to gaze upon the reflections of their own loveliness mirrored there. The reach of river—" from Nashawtuc to the Cliff"—above the confluence of the two branches was most beloved and frequented of Thoreau; here he sometimes brought Emerson, as on that summer evening when the sage's diary records, "the river-god took the form of my valiant Henry Thoreau and introduced me to the riches of his shadowy, starlit, moonlit stream," etc.

The deeper portion of the river near the Manse was Hawthorne's habitual resort for bathing and fishing, but his longer solitary voyages and his "wild, free .days" with Ellery Channing were upon the beautiful and sheltered North Branch,—the Assabeth of the "Mosses," —which flows into the Concord a half-mile above the Manse. Into this branch we turn our boat, and through sunshine and shade we follow the winsome course of the lingering stream, finding new and delightful seclusion at every turn. A railway now lies along one lofty bank, but its unsightliness is concealed by long lines of willows planted by the loving hands of poet and artist,—Bartlett and French,—and the infre- quent trains little disturb the seclusion of the place. Giant trees, standing with "their feet fixed in the flood," bend their bright foliage above the softly-flowing stream and fleck its surface with shadows; pond-lilies are still up-borne by its dreaming waters, and cardinal flowers bedeck its banks; its barer reaches are ribbons of reflected sky. The spot on the margin locally known as " The Hemlocks," and noted by Hawthorne as being only less sacred in his memory than the household hearth, remains itself undisturbed. Here a clump of great ever-greens projects from the base of the lofty bank above and across the stream, and forms on the shore a shaded bower, carpeted by the brown needles which have fallen through many a year. This was a favorite haunt of Hawthorne and Channing in blissful days; here they prepared their sylvan noontide feasts; here they lounged and dreamed; here their " talk gushed up like the babble of a fountain." As we recline in their accustomed resting-place beside the sighing stream, and look up at the azure heaven through the boughs where erstwhile often curled the smoke of their fire, we vainly try to imagine something of what would be the converse, merry or profound, of such starry spirits amid such an inspiring scene, and we more than ever regret that neither the gentle poet nor the subtle ro-mancer has chosen to share that converse with his readers.

A Storied River and Battle-Field

Long and lovingly we loiter in this consecrated spot, and then slowly float back to Hawthorne's landing-place by his orchard wall.

A few rods distant, at the corner of his field, is the site of the " rude bridge that arched the flood," and the first battle-ground of the American Revolution. On the farther side a colossal minute-man in bronze, modelled by the Concord sculptor French, surmounts a granite pedestal inscribed with Emerson's immortal epic, and marks the spot where stood the irregular array of the " embattled farmers" when they here " fired the shot heard round the world." The statue replaces a bush which sprang from the soil fertilized by the blood of Davis, and which Emerson imaged as the " burning bush where God spake for his people."

The position of the British regulars on the hither shore is indicated by the " votive stone" of Emerson's poem,—a slender obelisk of granite, —and near it, close under the wall of the Manse enclosure, is the rude memorial that marks the grave of the British soldiers who were slain on this spot. The current tradition that a lad who, after the battle, came, axe in hand, from the Manse wood-pile, found one of the soldiers yet alive and dispatched him with the axe, was first related to Hawthorne by James Russell Lowell, as they stood together above this grave. The effect of this story upon the feelings of the susceptible Hawthorne is told on a page of " The Old Manse," and—a score of years later and in different shape—is related in the romance of " Septimius Felton."

IV

THE HOME OF EMERSON

An Intellectual Capitol and Pharos — Its Grounds, Library, and Literary Workshop — Famous Rooms and Visitants — Relics and Reminiscences of the Concord Sage.

FOLLOWING the direction of the British retreat from the historic Common, we come, beyond the village, to the modest mansion which was for half a century the abode of the princely man who was not only " the Sage of Concord," but, in the esteem of some contemporaries, " was Concord itself."

Emerson declares, " great men never live in a crowd,"—" a scholar must embrace solitude as a bride, must have his glees and glooms alone." Of himself he says, " I am a poet and must therefore live in the country ; a sunset, a forest, a river view are more to me than many friends, and must divide my day with my books ;" and this was the consideration which finally determined his withdrawal from the storm and fret of the city to his chosen home here by Walden woods and among the scenes of his childhood. It was his retirement to this semi-seclusion which called forth his much-quoted poem, " Good-by, proud world ! I'm going home." To him here came the afflatus he had before lacked, here his faculties were inspirited, and here his literary productiveness commenced.

Behind a row of dense-leaved horse-chestnuts ranged along the highway, the quondam home of Emerson nestles among clustering evergreens which were planted by Bronson Alcott and Henry D. Thoreau for their friend. A copse of pines sighs in the summer wind close by; an orchard planted and pruned by Emerson's hands, and a garden tended by Thoreau, extend from the house to a brook flowing through the grounds and later joining the Concord by the famous old Manse; beyond the brook lies the way to Walden. At the left of the house is a narrow open reach of greensward on the farther verge of which erst stood the unique rustic bower —with a wind-harp of untrimmed branches above it—which was fashioned by the loving hands of Alcott. The mansion is a substantial, square, clapboarded structure of two stories, with hip-roofs; a square window projects at one side; a wing is joined at the back; covered porches protect the entrances; light paint covers the plain walls which gleam through the bowering foliage, and the whole aspect of the place is delightfully attractive and home-like. Its pleasant and unpretentious apartments more than realize the comfortable suggestion of the exterior. Adjoining the hall on the right is the plain, rectangular room which was the philosopher's library and workshop. The cheerful fireplace and the simple furnishings of the room are little changed since he here laid down his pen for the last time ; the heavy table held his manuscript, his books are ranged upon the shelves, the busts and portraits he cherished adorn the walls, his accustomed chair is upon the spot where he sat to write.

Emerson's afternoons were usually spent abroad, but his mornings were habitually passed among his books in this small corner-room— " the study under the pines"—recording, in " a pellucid style which his genius made classic," the truths which had come to him as he mused by shadowy lake or songful stream, in deep wood glade or wayside path. Most of all his pen produced, of divinest poetry, of gravest philosophy, of grandest thought, was minted into words and inscribed in this simple apartment.

The adjoining parlor—a spacious, pleasant, home-like room, furnished forth with many mementos of illustrious friends and guests—is scarcely less interesting than the library. This house was the intellectual capitol of the village ; to it freely came the Concord circle of shining ones,—Thoreau, Channing, Sanborn, the Alcotts, the Hoars,—less frequently, Hawthorne. For a long time Mrs. Samuel Ripley habitually passed her Sabbath evenings here. The Delphic Margaret Fuller, who was as truly the " blood of transcendentalism" as Emerson " was its brain," was here for months an honored guest. For long periods Thoreau, whose fame owes much to Emerson's generosity, was here an inmate and intimate. In Emerson's parlor were held the more formal *séances* of the Concord galaxy; here met the short-lived " Monday Evening Club," which George William Curtis whimsically describes as a " congress of oracles," who ate russet-apples and discoursed celestially while Hawthorne looked on from his corner,—" a statue of night and silence;" here were held many of Bronson Alcott's famous " conversations," as well as those of that disciple of Platonism, Dr. Jones.

Emerson belonged not to Concord only, but to the whole world,—" his thought was the thought of Christendom." To these plain rooms as to an intellectual court came, from his own and other lands, hundreds famed in art, literature, and politics. Here came Curtis and Bartol to sit at the feet of the sage; Charles Sumner and Moncure Conway to bear hence—as one of them has said—" memories like those Bunyan's pilgrim

must have cherished of the Interpreter." Here
' came Theodore Parker from the fight for free
thought," and Wendell Phillips and John Brown
from the conflict for free men ; here came Howells, bearing the line from Hawthorne, " I find
this young man worthy ;" here came Whittier,
Agassiz, Hedge, Longfellow, Bradford, Lowell,
Colonel Higginson, Elizabeth Peabody, Julia
Ward Howe, as to a fount of wisdom and purity.
In this unpretentious parlor have gathered such
guests as Stanley, Walt Whitman, Bret Harte,
Henry James, Louis Kossuth, Arthur Clough,
Lord Amberley, Jones Very, Fredrika Bremer,
Harriet Martineau, and many others who, like
these, would have felt repaid for their journey
over leagues of land and sea by a hand-clasp
and an hour's communion with the intellect that
has been the beacon of thousands in mental darkness and storm. With these came another class
of pilgrims, the great army of impracticables,
" men with long hair, long beards, long collars,—
many with long ears, each in full chase after the
millennium," and each intent upon securing the
endorsement of Emerson for his own pet scheme.
The wonder is that the little library saw any
work accomplished, so many came to it and
claimed the time of the master ; for to every
one—scholar, tradesman, and " crank"—were

accorded his never-failing courtesy and kindly interest. Any one might be the bearer of a divine message, so he listened to all,—the most uncouth and *outré* visitant might be the coming man for whom his faith waited, therefore all were admitted.

Here all were "assayed, not analyzed." Emerson's habitual quest for only the divinest traits and his quickened perception of the best in men enabled him to recognize excellencies which were yet unseen by others. While Hawthorne, the shy hermit at the Manse, was unheeded by the world and thought crazed by his neighbors, Emerson knew and proclaimed his transcendent genius. He first recognized the inspiration of Ellery Channing, and made for his exquisite verse exalted claims which have been fully justified, and which the world may yet allow. While to others Henry Thoreau was yet only an eccentric egotist, Emerson knew him as a poet and philosopher, and made him the "forest seer, the heart of all the scene," in his lyrical masterpiece "Wood-Notes." He promptly hailed Walt Whitman as a true poet while many of us were yet wondering if it were not charitable to think him insane.

Emerson's cordiality won for him the honor which prophets rarely enjoy in their own country;

the objects and places once associated with him here are still esteemed sacred by his old neighbors. We find among them at this day many who can know nothing of his books, but who, for memory of his simple kindness, go far from their furrow or swath to show us spots he loved and frequented in woodland or meadow, on swelling hill-side or by winding river.

To his home here Emerson brought his bride sixty years ago; here he lived his fruitful life and accomplished his work; here he rose to the zenith of poesy and prophecy; to him here came the "great and grave transition which may not king or priest or conqueror spare;" from here his wife, lingering behind him in the eternal march, went a year or two ago to rejoin him on the piny hill-top; and here his unmarried daughter—of "saint-like face and nun-like garb"—inhabits his home and cherishes its treasures.

Emerson's son and biographer some time ago relinquished his medical practice in Concord, and has since devoted himself to art. He has a residence a mile or so out of the village, but spends much of his time abroad. Last year he lectured in London upon the lives and writings of some of the Concord authors.

THE ORCHARD HOUSE AND ITS NEIGHBORS

A PLAIN little cottage by the road, not far from Emerson's home, was for some time the abode of the companion of many of his rambles through the countryside, — the poet Ellery Channing. It was to this simple dwelling, as the author of " Little Women" once told the writer, that Channing brought his young wife —sister of Margaret Fuller—before the Alcotts had come to live in their hill-side home under the wooded ridge, and it was here he commenced the sequestered life so suited to his nature and tastes.

Some of his descriptive poems of Concord landscapes were written in this little cottage. The scenes of one of his earlier winters in the neighborhood—when he chopped wood in a rude clearing—are portrayed in the exquisite lines of his " Woodman." In those days he thought his poems " too sacred to be sold for money," and they were kept for his circle of friends. Of the poet's modest home Miss Fuller—that "dazzling woman with the flame in her heart"—was a frequent inmate; it was from Concord that she went to live in the family of Horace Greeley in New York. At the time of her visits at Channing's cottage Thoreau was sojourning with Emerson, and we may be sure that the quartette of starry souls, thus *juxtaposé*, held much soulful and edifying converse. But those of us who deplore our lack of the supreme transcendental spirit which we ascribe to the Concord circle may find consolation in reflecting that some of this gifted company had also earthly tastes, and found even discourse concerning the " over-soul" sometimes tiresome. The " strained pitch of intellectual intensity" was, upon occasion, gladly relaxed; thus we discover the exalted Channing sometime profanely inviting Hawthorne — " the gentlest man that kindly Nature ever drew" — to visit him in Concord, alluring the novelist with prospects of strong-waters, pipes and tobacco without end, and urging, as the utmost inducement, " Emerson is gone and there is nobody here to bore you."

A few furlongs farther eastward, under the high-soaring elms of the Lexington road, we

come to the "Orchard House" of Bronson Alcott, "the grandfather of the 'Little Women.'"
The tasteful dwelling stands several rods back
from the street, nestling cosily at the foot of a
pine-crowned slope, and having a wide, sunny
outlook in front. Embowered in orchards and
vines, and shaded by the overreaching arms of
giant elms, it seems a most delightful home for
culture and contemplative study. The cottage
itself is a low, wide, gabled, picturesquely irregular edifice, which our Pythagorean mystic
evolved from a forlorn, box-like farm-house
which he found here when he purchased the
place. The rustic fence he set along the highway is replaced by an ambitious modern structure.
On this hill-side Alcott, the "most transcendent
of the transcendentalists," lived for nearly thirty
years,—but not all of that time in this house,—
coming here first after the failure of his "Fruit-
lands" community in 1845, and finally twelve
years later. Prior to this he had been assisted
by Margaret Fuller and Elizabeth Peabody in
his renowned Boston Temple School, which was
a failure in a financial sense only, since it furnished a theme for Miss Peabody's "Record of
a School," and Louisa Alcott's girlish recollections of it provided her a model for the delightful "Plumfield" of her books.

The Orchard House and its Neighbors

Alcott's treatise on "Early Education," his "Gospels" and "Orphic Sayings," had been published, and his "very best contribution to literature"—his daughter Louisa—was also extant before he came to this home, but it was here that his maturer works and most of his charming essays and "Conversations" were produced.

In this house were held the early sessions of the Summer School of Philosophy, of which Alcott was the leading spirit; here his daughter, the "Beth" of "Jo's" books, died. The interior of the "Orchard House" is roomy and quaint and abounds in surprising nooks and cosy recesses. In the corner-room Louisa wrote "Little Women" and other delicious books; in the room behind it, May, "our Madonna," —who died Madame Nieriker,—had her studio and practised the art which made her famous before her untimely end. In the great attic under the sloping roof the "Little Women" acted the "comic tragedies" written by "Jo" and "Meg" (some of them now published in a volume with a "Foreword" by "Meg") until the increasing audiences of Concord children caused the removal of the mimic stage to the big barn on the hill-side.

Hawthorne makes this house the abode of Robert Hagburn in "Septimius Felton." Along the brow of the tree-clad ridge which overlooks the place, and to which Bronson Alcott resorted for the morning and evening view, the patriots hastened to intercept the retreat of the British troops, "blackened and bloody." In the depression of the ridge just back of the house we find the spot where "Septimius Felton" shot the young officer, Cyril Norton, and buried him under the trees. On the grave here "Septimius" sat with Rose Garfield and the half-crazed Sibyl Dacy; here grew the crimson flower which he distilled in his "elixir of immortality," and here Sibyl came to die after her draught of the compound.

After the removal of the Alcotts to the Thoreau house in the village, "Apple Slump"—as Louisa sometimes called this orchard home— became the property and residence of that disciple of Hegel, Professor Harris,—once principal of the Summer School of Philosophy, and now the head of the National Bureau of Education at Washington,—who sometimes comes here in summer.

The "Hillside Chapel," erected by Mrs. Elizabeth Thompson, of New York, for the sessions of the Summer Philosophers, is placed among the trees of the orchard adjoining Alcott's old home. It is a plain little structure of wood, tasteful in design, with pointed gables and vine-draped porch and windows. Its embowered walls, unpainted and unplastered, seem " scarcely large enough to contain the wisdom of the world," but they have held assemblages of such lights as Emerson, Alcott, Sanborn, Bartol, McCosh, Holland, Porter, Lathrop, Stedman, Wilder, Hedge, Dr. Jones, Elizabeth Peabody, Ward Howe, Ednah Cheney, and other like seekers and promoters of fundamental truth.

VI

HAWTHORNE'S WAYSIDE HOME.

Sometime Abode of Alcott—Hawthorne—Lathrop—Margaret Sidney—Storied Apartments—Hawthorne's Study—His Mount of Vision—Where Septimius Felton and Rose Garfield dwelt.

ON the Lexington road, a little way beyond the Orchard House, is the once Wayside home of Hawthorne, the dwelling in which, at a tender age, Louisa M. Alcott made her first literary essay. It is a curious, wide, straggling, and irregular structure, of varying ages, heights, and styles. The central gambrel-roofed portion was the original house of four rooms, described as the residence of "Septimius Felton;" other rooms have been added at different periods and to serve the need of successive occupants, until an architecturally incongruous and altogether delightful mansion has been produced. To the ugly little square house which Alcott found here in 1845 and christened "Hillside" he added a low wing at each side, the central gable in the front of the old roof, and wide rustic piazzas across the front of the wings. No additions were made during Hawthorne's first residence here, nor during the occupancy of Mrs. Hawthorne's brother, while the novelist was abroad; but when Hawthorne returned to it in 1860, with "most of his family twice as big as when they left," he enlarged one wing by adding the barn to it, heightened the other side-wing, erected two spacious apartments at the back, and crowned the edifice with a square third-story study, which, with its great chimney and many gables, overtops the rambling roofs like an observatory, and may have been suggested by the tower of the Villa Montauto, where he wrote "The Marble Faun." No important changes have been made by the subsequent owners of the place.

Hawthorne's widow left the Wayside in 1868. It was afterward occupied by a school for young ladies; then by Hawthorne's daughter Rose— herself a charming writer—with her husband, the gifted and versatile George Parsons Lathrop; later it was purchased by the Boston publisher Daniel Lothrop, and has since been the summer home of his widow, who is widely known as " Margaret Sidney," the creator of " Five Little Peppers," and writer of many delightful books. Hawthorne said, anent his visit to Abbotsford, " A house is forever ruined as a home by having been the abode of a great man,"—a truth well attested by the present amiable mistress of his own Wayside, whose experience with a legion of unaccredited, intrusive, and often insolent persons who come at all hours of the day, and sometimes in the night, demanding to be shown over the place, would be more ludicrous were it less provoking.

Some details of the interior have been beautified by the æsthetic taste of Mrs. Lothrop, but an appreciative reverence for Hawthorne leads her to preserve his home and its belongings essentially unchanged. At the right of the entrance is an antique reception-room, which was Hawthorne's study during his first residence here, as it had long before been the study of "Septimius Felton" in the tale. It is a low-studded apartment with floor of oaken planks, heavy beams strutting from its ceiling, a generous fireplace against a side wall, and with two windows looking out upon the near highway. In this room Hawthorne wrote "Tanglewood Tales" and "Life of Franklin Pierce;" and here that creature of his imagination, "Septimius," brooded over his doubts and questions. Through yonder windows "Septimius" saw the British soldiery pass and repass; above this oaken mantel—now artistically fitted and embellished with rare pottery—he hung the sword of the officer he had slain; before this fireplace he pored over the mysterious manuscript his dying victim had given him; on this hearth he distilled the mystic potion, and here poor Sibyl quaffed it. The spacious room at the left, across the hall, was at first Hawthorne's parlor; but after he enlarged the dwelling this became the library, where he read aloud to the assembled family on winter evenings, and where his widow afterward transcribed his " Note-Books" for publication. The sunny room above this was the chamber of the unfortunate Una; Hawthorne's own sleeping apartment, on the second floor, is entered from the hall through the narrowest of door-ways. In the upper hall a little wall-closet was the repository of Hawthorne's manuscripts, and here, to the surprise of all, an entire unpublished romance was found after his death. From this hall a narrow stairway, so steep that one need cling to the iron rail at the side in order to scale it, ascends to Hawthorne's study in the tower, a lofty room with vaulted ceiling. On one side wall is the Gothic enclosure of the stairs, against which once stood his plain oaken writing-desk; upon it the bronze inkstand he brought from Italy, where it held the ink for " The Marble Faun." In this inkstand, he declared, lurked " the little imp" which sometimes controlled his pen. Attached to a side of the staircase was the high desk or shelf upon which he often wrote standing. Book-closets filled the corners at the back, and a little fireplace with a plain mantel was placed between two of the windows. Loving hands have neatly decorated the ceiling, and painted upon the walls mottoes commemorative of the master who wrought here. The views he beheld through the windows of this sanctum when he lifted his eyes from his book or manuscript are tranquil and soothing : across his roofs in one direction he looked upon the sunny grasslands of the valley; in another he saw placid slopes of darkly-wooded hills and a reach of the elm-bordered road ; in a third direction, smiling fields and the vineyards where the famous Concord grape first grew met his vision ; and through his north windows appeared the thick woods that crowned his own hill-top,—so near that he " could see the nodding wild flowers" among the trees and breathe the woodland odors.

Local tradition declares that, to prevent intrusion into this den, Hawthorne habitually sat upon a trap-door in the floor, which was the only entrance. Without this precaution he found in this eyrie the seclusion he coveted, and here, among the birds and the tree-tops, remote from the tumult of life and above ordinary distracting influences, he could linger undisturbed in that border-land between shadow and substance which was his delight, could evoke and fix upon his pages the weird creatures of his fancy. Several hours of each day he passed here alone in musing or composition, and here, besides some papers for the " Atlantic," he wrote " Our Old Home," " Grimshaw's Secret," " Septimius Felton," and the " Dolliver Romance" fragment. Years before, Thoreau told him, the Wayside had once been inhabited by a man who believed he would never die. The thus suggested idea, of a deathless man associated with this house, seems to have clung to Hawthorne in his last years, and was embodied in both his later works,—the scene of " Septimius Felton" being laid here at the Wayside. No one knew aught of its composition, and the author, rereading the tale in the solitude of this study and finding it in some way lacking the perfection of his ideal, laid it away in his closet, and, in weariness and failing health, commenced and vainly tried to finish the " Dolliver Romance" from the same materials.

The house is separated from the highway by a narrow strip of sward, out of which grow elms planted by Bronson Alcott and clustering evergreens rooted by Hawthorne himself. The greater part of his domain lies along the dark slope and the wooded summit of the ridge which rises close behind the house. At the extremity of the grounds nearest the Orchard House, a depression in the turf marks the site of the little house where dwelt the Rose Garfield of "Septimius." Hawthorne planted sunflowers in this hollow, and Julian, his son, remembers seeing the novelist stand here and contemplate their wide disks above the old cellar.

On the steep hill-side remain the rough terraces Alcott fashioned when he occupied the place, and many of the flowering locusts and fruit-trees he and Thoreau planted. Here, too, are the sombre spruces and firs which Hawthorne sent from "Our Old Home" or planted after his return, and all are grown until they overshadow the whole place and fairly embower the house with their branches. Along the hill-side are the famous "Acacia path" of Mrs. Hawthorne and other walks planned by the novelist, some of them having been opened by him in the last summer of his life. By one path, once familiar to his feet, we find our way up the steep ascent among the locusts to the "Mount of Vision,"— as Mrs. Hawthorne named the ridge to which the novelist daily resorted for study and meditation.

The hill-top is clothed with a tangled growth of trees which hides it from the lower world and renders it a fitting trysting-place for the wizard romancer and the mystic figures which abound in his tales. Along the brow we trace, among the ferns, vestiges of the pathway worn by his feet. In the safe seclusion of this spot he spent delectable hours, lying under the trees " with a book in his hands and an unwritten book in his thoughts," while the pines murmured to him of the mystery and shadow he loved. More often he sat on a rustic seat between yonder pair of giant trees, or paced his foot-path hour after hour, as he pondered his plots and worked out the mystic details of many romances, some of them never to be written. Walking here with Fields he unfolded his design of the " Dolliver" tale, which he left half told. Here he composed the weird story of " Septimius Felton," while trudging on the very path he describes as having been worn by his hero,—Hawthorne himself habitually walking, with hands clasped behind him and with eyes bent on the ground, in the very attitude he ascribes to " Septimius" as Rose saw him " treading, treading, treading, many a year," on this foot-path by the grave of the officer he had slain. In this refuge Hawthorne remained a whole day alone with his grief, when tidings came to him of the loss of his sister in the burning of the " Henry Clay."

Here he sat with Howells one memorable afternoon. In the last years his wife was often with
him here, sometimes walking, but more frequently sitting, with him,—as did Rose with
"Septimius,"—and looking out, through an
opening in the foliage near the western end of
his path, upon the restful landscape, not less
charming to-day than when his eyes lovingly
lingered upon it. We see the same broad, sun-
kissed meadows awave with lush grass and flecked
with fleeting cloud-shadows, and beyond, the dark
forests of Thoreau's Walden and the gentle outlines of low-lying hills which shut in the valley
like a human life.

For some months after the election to the
Presidency of his friend Franklin Pierce, the
Wayside was frequented by office-seekers; but
ordinarily Hawthorne had few visitors besides
his Concord friends. Fields, Holmes, Hilliard,
Whipple, Longfellow, Howells, Horatio Bridge,
the poet Stoddard, Henry Bright, came to him
here. The visits of "Gail Hamilton" (Miss
Abigail Dodge), mentioned by Hawthorne as
"a sensible, healthy-minded woman," were especially enjoyed by him. His own visits were
very infrequent; "Orphic" Alcott said that in
the several years he lived next door Hawthorne
came but twice into his house: the first time he

quickly excused himself " because the stove was too hot," next time " because the clock ticked too loud."

The Wayside was the only home Hawthorne ever owned. To it he came soon after his removal from the " little red house" in Berkshire, and to it he returned from his sojourn abroad; here, with failing health and desponding spirits, he lived in the gloomy war-days,—writing in his study or, with steps more and more uncertain, pacing his hill-top; from here he set out with his life-long friend Pierce on the last sad journey which ended so quickly and quietly.

VII

THE WALDEN OF THOREAU

A Transcendental Font—Emerson's Garden—Thoreau's Cove—Cairn—Beanfield—Resort of Emerson—Hawthorne—Channing—Hosmer—Alcott, etc.

ONE long-to-be-remembered day we follow the shady foot-paths, once familiar to the sublimated Concord company, through their favorite forest retreats to " the blue-eyed Walden,"—sung by many a bard, beloved by transcendental saint and seer. After a delightful stroll of a mile or more, we emerge from the wood and see the lovely lakelet " smiling upon its neighbor pines." We find it a half-mile in diameter, with bold and picturesquely irregular margins indented with deep bays and mostly wooded to the pebbles at the water's edge. From this setting of emerald foliage it scintillates like a gem : its wavelets lave a narrow pebbly shore within which a bottom of pure white sand gleams upward through the most transparent water ever seen. At one point where the railway skirts the margin, the woods are disfigured with pavilions and tables for summer pleasure-seekers, and a farther wooded slope has recently been ravaged by fire ; but most of the shore has escaped both

68

profanation and devastation, so that the literary pilgrim will find the shrines he seeks little disturbed since the Concord luminaries here had their haunt.

From the summit of the forest ledge which rises from the southern shore, the lakelet seems a foliage-framed patch of the firmament. This rocky eminence affords a wide and enchanting prospect, and was the terminus and object of many excursions of Emerson and the other "Walden-Pond-Walkers," as the transcendentalists were styled by their more prosy and orthodox neighbors. It was upon this elevation in the midst of a portion of his estate which he celebrates in his poetry as "My Garden"—whose "banks slope down to the blue lake-edge"— that Emerson proposed to erect a lodge or retreat for retirement and thought. A mossy path, once trodden almost daily by the philosopher and his friends, brings us to the beautiful and secluded cove where Emerson and Thoreau kept a boat, and where the shining ones often came to bathe in this limpid water. Ablution here seems to have been a sort of transcendent baptism, and many a visitor, eminent in art, thought, or letters, has boasted that he walked and talked with Emerson in Walden woods and bathed with him in Walden water. In this romantic nook Thoreau spent much time during his hermitage, sitting in reverie on its banks or afloat on its glassy surface, fishing or playing his flute to the charmed perch. On the shore of this cove he procured the stones for the foundations and the sand for the plastering of his cabin. From the water's edge an obscure path, bordered by the wild flowers he loved, winds among the murmuring pines up to the site of Thoreau's retreat, on a gentle hill-side which falls away to the shore a few rods distant. A cairn of small stones, placed by reverent pilgrims, stands upon or near the spot where he erected his dwelling at an outlay of twenty-eight dollars and lived upon an income of one dollar per month.

The hermit would hardly know the place now; his young pines are grown into giants that allow but glimpses of the shimmering lake; even the "potato hole" he dug under his cabin, whence the squirrels chirped at him from beneath the floor as he sat to write, and where he kept his winter store,—the "beans with the weevil in them" and the "potatoes with every third one nibbled by chipmunks,"—is obliterated and overgrown with the glabrous sumach. His nearby field, where he learned to "know beans" and gathered relics of a previous and aboriginal race of bean-hoers, is covered by a growth of pines and dwarf oaks, in places so dense as to be almost impassable.

Some one has said, " Thoreau experienced Nature as other men experience religion." Certainly the life at Walden, which he depicted in one of the most fascinating of books, was in all its details—whether he was ecstatically hoeing beans in his field or dreaming on his door-step, floating on the lake or rambling in forest and field—that of an ascetic and devout worshipper of Nature in all her moods. Thoreau " built himself in Walden woods a den" in 1845,—after his return from tutoring in the family of Emerson's brother at Staten Island; here he wrote most of " Walden" and the " Week on the Concord and Merrimac Rivers," and much more that has been posthumously published; from here he went to jail for refusing to pay a tax on his poll, from here he made the excursion described in " The Maine Woods."

He finally removed from Walden in the autumn of 1847, to reside in the house of Emerson during that sage's absence in Europe. An old neighbor of Thoreau's, who had often watched his " stumpy" figure as he hoed the beans, and had even once or twice assisted him in that celestial agriculture, tells us that Thoreau's hut was removed by a gardener to the middle of the beanfield and there occupied for some years. Later it was purchased by a farmer, who set it upon wheels and conveyed it to his farm some miles distant, where it has decayed and gone to pieces.

In Concord it is not difficult to identify the personages associated with Thoreau's life at Walden Pond and referred to in his book. The "landlord and waterlord" of the domain, on which Thoreau was "a squatter," was Waldo Emerson; the owner of the axe which the hermit borrowed to hew the frame of his hut was Bronson Alcott; the "honorable raisers" of the structure were Emerson, Curtis the Nile "Howadji," Alcott, Hosmer, and others; the lady who made the sketch of the hermitage which appears on the title-page of "Walden" was the author's sister Sophia. Of the hermit's visitors here, "the one who came oftenest" was Emerson; "the one who came farthest" was also the poet whom the hermit "took to board for a fortnight," Ellery Channing; the "long-headed farmer," who had "donned a frock instead of a professor's gown," was Thoreau's neighbor and life-long friend Edmund Hosmer, who is celebrated in the poetry of Emerson and Channing; the "last of the philosophers," the "Great Looker—great Expecter," who "first peddled wares and then his own brains," was Bronson Alcott, who spent long evenings here in converse with the hermit, or in listening to chapters from his manuscript. Here came Hawthorne to talk with his " cast-iron man" about trees and arrow-heads ; here came George Hilliard and James T. Fields, and others,—sometimes so many that the hut would scarce contain them ; the only com-plaint heard from Thoreau anent the narrow-ness of his quarters being that there was not room for the words to ricochet between him and his guests. Here, too, came humbler visitors, hunted slaves, who were never denied the shelter of the hermitage nor the sympathy and aid of the hermit.

Another generation of visitors comes now to this spot,—pilgrims from far, like ourselves, to the shrine of a " stoic greater than Zeno or Xenophanes,"—a man whose " breath and core was conscience." We linger till the twilight, for the genius of this shrine seems very near us as we muse in the place where he dwelt incar-nate alone with Nature, and there is for us a hint of his healthful spirit in the odor of his pines and of the wild flowers beside his path,—a vague whisper of his earnest, honest thought in the murmur of the clustering boughs and in the lap-ping of the wavelets upon the mimic strand.

The Concord Pilgrimage

We bring from the shore a stone—the whitest we can find—for his cairn, and place with it a bright leaf, like those his callers in other days left for visiting cards upon his door-step, and then, through the wondrous half-lights of the summer evening, we walk silently away.

VIII

THE HILL-TOP HEARSED
WITH PINES

DURING Hawthorne's habitation of the
"Old Manse" and his first residence at
the Wayside, his favorite walk was to the
"Sleepy Hollow," a beautifully diversified
precinct of hill and vale which lies a little
way eastward from the village. His habitual
resting-place here was a pine-shaded hill-top
where he often met Emerson, Thoreau, Bronson Alcott, Elizabeth Hoar, Mrs. Ripley, or
Margaret Fuller,—for all that sublimated company loved and frequented this spot. More
often Hawthorne lounged and mused or chatted
here alone with his lovely wife. Their letters
and journals of this period make frequent mention of the walks to this place and of "our
castle,"—a fanciful structure which, in their
happy converse here under the pines, they
planned to erect for their habitation on this
hill-top. In their pleasant conceit, the terraced
path which skirts the verge of the hollow and
thence ascends the ridge was the grand " chariot-

road" to their castle. This park has become a cemetery,—at its dedication Emerson made an oration and Frank B. Sanborn read a beautiful ode,—and on their beloved hill-top nearly all the transcendent company whom Hawthorne used to meet there, save Margaret Fuller who rests beneath the sea, lie at last in "the dreamless sleep that lulls the dead."

First came Thoreau, to lie among his kindred under the wild flowers and the fallen needles of his dear pines, in a grave marked now by a simple stone graven with his name and age. Next came Hawthorne: with his "half-told tale" and a wreath of apple-blossoms from the "Old Manse" resting on his coffin, and with Emerson, Longfellow, Fields, Ellery Channing, Agassiz, Hoar, Lowell, Whipple, Alcott, Holmes, and George Hilliard walking mournfully by his side, he was borne, through the flowering orchards and up the hill-side path,—which was to have been his "chariot-road,"—to a grave on the site of the "castle" of his fancy; where his dearest friend Franklin Pierce covered him with flowers and James Freeman Clarke committed his mortal part to the lap of earth. Alas, that the beloved cohabitant of his dream-castle must lie in death a thousand leagues away! in no dream of his would such a separation from her have seemed possible. She tried to mark his tomb by a leafy monument of hawthorn shrubbery, but the rigorous climate prevented; now a low marble, inscribed with the one word "Hawthorne," stands at either extremity of his grave, and a glossy growth of periwinkle covers the spot where sleeps the great master of American romance. Some smaller graves are beside his: in one lies a child of Julian Hawthorne; in another, Rose—the daughter of Hawthorne's age—laid the son which her husband, Parsons Lathrop, commemorates in the lines of "The Flown Soul." Next Mrs. Ripley and Elizabeth Hoar were borne to this "God's acre," and then Emerson—followed by a vast concourse and mourned by all the world—was brought to "give his body back to earth again," in this loved retreat, near Hawthorne and his own "forest-seer" Thoreau. A gigantic pine towers above him here, and a massive triangular boulder of untooled pink quartz—already marred by the vandalism of relic-seekers—is placed to mark the grave of the great "King of Thought." It bore no inscription or device of any sort until a few months ago, when a bronze plate inscribed with his name and years and the lines—

"The passive master lent his hand
To the vast soul that o'er him planned"—

77

was set in the rough surface of the stone. By Emerson lie his wife, his mother, two children of his son and biographer Dr. Emerson, and his own little child,—the " wondrous, deep-eyed boy" whom Emerson mourned in his matchless " Threnody."

> " O child of paradise,
>   Boy who made dear his father's home,
>   In whose deep eyes
>   Men read the welfare of the times to come,—
>   I am too much bereft."

Six years after Emerson, Bronson Alcott and his illustrious daughter Louisa were laid here, within a few yards of Hawthorne and the rest, on a spot selected by the " Beth" of the Alcott books who was herself the first to be interred in it. Now all the " Little Women" repose here with their parents and good " John Brooke,"— " Jo" being so placed as to suggest to her biographer that she is still to take care of parents and sisters " as she had done all her life."

No other spot of earth holds dust more precious than does this " hill-top hearsed with pines." We are pleased to find the native beauty of the place little disturbed,—the trees, the indigenous grasses, ferns, and flowers remaining for the most part as they were known and

The Hill-top Hearsed with Pines

loved by those who sleep beneath them. The contour of the ground and the foliage which clusters upon the slopes measurably shut out the view of other portions of the enclosure from this secluded hill-top, and, as we sit by the graves under the moaning pines, we seem to be alone with these *our* dead. Through the boughs we have glimpses of the motionless deeps of a summer sky ; the patches of sunshine which illumine the graves about us are broken by foliate shadows sometimes as still as if painted upon the turf. No discordant sound from the haunts of men disturbs our meditations ; the silence is unbroken save by the frequent sighs of the mourning pines.

As we linger, the pervading quiet becomes something more than mere silence, it acquires the air and sense of reserve : the impression is borne into our thought that these asleep here, who once freely gave us their richest and best, are withholding something from us now,—some newly-learned wisdom, some higher thought. Does "an awful spell bind them to silence," or are they vainly repeating to us in the tender monotone of the pines a message we cannot hear or cannot bear ? Or have they ceased from all ken or care for earthly things ? Do they no longer love this once beloved spot ? Do they not rejoice in the beauty of this summer

day and the sunshine that falls upon their win-
dowless palace? Are they conscious of our
reverent tread on the turf above them, of our
low words of remembrance and affection? Do
they care that we have come from far to bend
over them here?

" For knowledge of all these things, we must"
—as the greatest of this transcendent circle once
said—" wait for to-morrow morning."

IN AND OUT OF LITERARY BOSTON

IN BOSTON

OUT OF BOSTON

IN BOSTON

A Golden Age of Letters—Literary Associations—Isms—Clubs—Where Hester Prynne and Silas Lapham lived—The Corner Book-store—Home of Fields—Sargent—Hilliard—Aldrich—Deland—Parkman—Holmes—Howells—Moulton—Hale—Howe—Jane Austin, etc.

OF the cisatlantic cities our "modern Athens" is, to the literary pilgrim, the most interesting; for, whatever may be the claims of other cities to the present literary primacy, all must concede that Boston was long the intellectual capital of the continent and its centre of literary culture and achievement. If the pilgrim have attained to middle life and be loyal to the literary idols of his youth, his regard for the Boston of to-day must be largely reminiscential of a past that is rapidly becoming historic; for, of the constellation of brilliant authors and thinkers who first gained for the place its pre-eminence in letters, few or none remain alive. The requirements of labor and trade are transforming the old streets; the sedate and comfortable dwellings, once the abodes or the resorts of the *littérateurs*, are giving place to palatial shops or great factories; the neighborhood where Bancroft, Choate, Winthrop, Webster, and Edward Everett dwelt within a

few rods of each other was long ago surrendered to merchandise and mammon; yet for us
the busy scenes are haunted by memories and
peopled by presences which the spirit of trade
is powerless to exorcise.

To tread the streets which have daily echoed
the foot-falls of the illustrious company who
created here a golden age of learning and culture were alone a pleasure, but the city holds
many closer and more personal mementos of
her dead prophets, as well as the homes of a
present generation who worthily strive to sustain
her place and prestige.

Interwoven with the older Boston are literary
associations hardly less memorable and enduring
than its history: in the belfry of its historic
holy of holies—Old South Church—was the
study of the historian Dr. Belknap, and the
dove that nested beneath the church-bell is preserved in the poetry of N. P. Willis; King's
Chapel, the sanctuary where the beloved Dr.
Holmes worshipped for so many years, and
whence he was not long ago sadly borne to his
burial, figures in the fiction of Fenimore Cooper;
historic Copp's Hill is also a scene in a tale of
the same novelist; the court-house occupies the
site of the "beetle-browed" prison of Hester
Prynne of "The Scarlet Letter;" the storied old

In Boston

State-house marked the place of her pillory; the theatre of the Boston Massacre is the scene of the thrilling episode of Hawthorne's " Gray Champion;" his " Legends of Province House" commemorate the ancient structure which stood nearly opposite the Old South Church; the Tremont House, where the "Jacobins' Club" used to assemble with Ripley, Channing, Theodore Parker, Bronson Alcott, Peabody, and the extreme reformers, was the resort of Hawthorne's " Miles Coverdale," as it was of the novelist himself, and on the street here he saw " ragamuffin Moodie" of " The Blithedale Romance." On the site of Bowdoin School, Charles Sumner was born; at one hundred and twenty Hancock Street he lived and composed the early orations which made his fame; at number one Exeter Place, Theodore Parker, the Vulcan of the New England pulpit, forged his bolts and wrote the " Discourses of Religion;" in Essex Street lived and wrote Wendell Phillips, at thirty-seven Common Street he died; at thirty-one Hollis Street the gifted Harriet Martineau was the guest of Francis Jackson; at the corner of Congress and Water Streets Lloyd Garrison wrote and published " The Liberator." In this older city, antedating the luxury of the Back Bay district of the new Boston, Mather wrote

the "Magnalia," Paine sang his songs, Allston
composed his tales, Buckminster wrote his homilies, Bowditch translated La Place's "*Mécanique
céleste.*" Here Emerson, Motley, Parkman,
and Poe were born; here Bancroft lived, Combe
wrote, Spurzheim died. Here Maffit, Channing, and Pierpont preached; Agassiz, Phillips,
and Lyell lectured; Alcott, Elizabeth Peabody,
and Fuller taught. Here Sargent wrote "Deal-
ings with the Dead," Sprague his "Curiosity,"
Prescott his "Ferdinand and Isabella;" here
Margaret Fuller held the "Conversations" which
attracted and impressed the leading spirits of the
time, and Bronson Alcott favored elect circles
with his Orphic and oracular utterances; here
lived Melvill, pictured in Holmes's "Last Leaf;"
here Emerson preached Unitarianism "until he
had carried it to the jumping-off-place," as one of
his quondam parishioners avers, and here commenced his career as philosopher and lecturer.
Here, besides those above mentioned, Dwight,
Brisbane, Quincy, Ripley, Graham, Thompson,
Hovey, Loring, Miller, Mrs. Folsom, and others
of similar ability or zeal, discoursed and wrote
in advocacy of the various reforms and "isms"
in vogue half a century or more ago.

It has been said that, according to the local
creed, whoso is born in Boston needs not to be

born again, but some decades ago a literary prowler, like ourselves, discovered that " nobody is born in Boston," the people who have made its fame in letters and art being usually allured to it from other places. This is true in less degree of the present age, since Hale, Robert Grant, Ballou,—of " The Pearl of India,"—Bates, Guiney, Elizabeth Stuart Phelps, and others are " to the manor born ;" but, if Boston has few birthplaces, she cherishes the homes and haunts of two generations of adult intellectual giants.

Prominent among the literary landmarks is the " Corner Book-store"—once the shop of the father of Dr. Clarke—at School and Washington Streets, which, like Murray's in London, has long been the rendezvous of the *littérateurs.* Here appeared the first American edition of " The Opium Eater" and of Tennyson's poems. Here was the early home of the " Atlantic," then edited by James T. Fields, who was the literary partner of the firm and the presiding genius of the old store. This lover of letters and sympathetic friend of literary men—always kind of heart and generous of hand—drew to him here the foremost of that galaxy who first achieved for America a place in the world of letters. To this literary Rialto, as familiar loungers, came in that golden age George Hilliard, Emerson, Ticknor, Saxe, Whipple, Longfellow, Hawthorne, Lowell, Agassiz, the "Autocrat," and the rest, to loiter among and discuss the new books, or, more often, to chat with their friend Fields at his desk, in the nook behind the green baize curtain. The store is altered some since Fields left it; the curtained back-corner, which was the domain of the Celtic urchin "Michael Angelo" and the trysting spot of the literary fraternity, has given place to shelves of shining books. The side entrance—used mostly by the authors because it brought them more directly to Fields's desk and den—is replaced by a window which looks out upon the spot where, as we remember with a thrill, Fields last shook Hawthorne's hand and stood looking after him as—faltering with weakness—he walked up this side street with Pierce to start upon the journey from which he never returned.

Literary tourists come to the store as to a shrine: thus in later years Matthew Arnold, Cable, Edmund Gosse, Professor Drummond, Dr. Doyle, and others like them, have visited the old corner. Nor is it deserted by the authors of the day; Holmes was often here up to the time of his death, and the visitor may still see, turning the glossy pages, some who are writers as well as readers of books : Thomas Bailey Aldrich, Scudder, Alger, Robert Grant,—whose "Reflections" and "Opinions" have been so widely read,—Miss Winthrop, Miss Jewett, Mrs. Louise Chandler Moulton, and Mrs. Coffin are among those who still come to the familiar place. Near by, in Washington Street, Hawthorne's first romance, "Fanshawe," was published in 1828. From Fields's famous store the transition to the staid old mansion which was long his home, and in which his widow still lives, is easy and natural. We find it pleasantly placed below the western slope of Beacon Hill, overlooking an enchanting prospect of blue waters and sunset skies. It is one of those dignified, substantial, and altogether comfortable dwellings—with spacious rooms, wide halls, easy stairways, and generous fireplaces—which we inherit from a previous generation. Here Fields, hardly less famed as an author than as the friend of authors, and his gifted wife—who is still a charming writer—created in their beautiful home an atmosphere which attracted to it the best and highest of their kind, and made it what it has been for more than forty years, a centre and ganglion of literary life and interest. The old-fashioned rooms are aglow with most precious memories and teem with artistic and literary treasures, many of them being *souvenirs* of the illustrious authors whom the Fields have numbered among their friends and guests. The letters of Dickens, Hawthorne, Emerson, and others reveal the quality of the hospitality of this house and show how it was prized by its recipients. For years this was the Boston home of Hawthorne; to it came Emerson, Longfellow, and Whittier almost as freely as to their own abodes; here Holmes, Lowell, Charles Sumner, Greene, Bayard Taylor, Joseph Jefferson, were frequent guests; and here we see a quaintly furnished bedchamber which has at various times been occupied by Dickens, Trollope, Arthur Clough, Thackeray, Charles Kingsley, Matthew Arnold, Charlotte Cushman, and others of equal fame. Of the delights of familiar intercourse with the starry spirits who frequented this house, of their brilliant discussions of men and books, their scintillations of wit, their sage and sober words of wisdom, Mrs. Annie Fields affords but tantalizing hints in her reminiscences and the glimpses she occasionally allows us of her husband's diary and letters. Fields's library on the second floor—described as " My Friend's Library"—is a most alluring apartment, where we see, besides the " Shelf of Old Books" of which Mrs. Fields gives such a sympathetic account, other shelves containing numerous curious and uniquely precious volumes,—among them the few hundreds of worn and much annotated books which constituted the library of Leigh Hunt. In this room Emerson, while awaiting breakfast, wrote one of his poems, to which the hostess gave title.

In later years a younger generation of writers came to this mansion: Celia Thaxter was a frequent guest; the princess-like Sarah Orne Jewett, beloved by Whittier as a daughter, has made it her Boston home; Aldrich comes to see the widow of his friend; Miss Preston, Mrs. Ward, and other luminous spirits may be met among the company who assemble in these memory-haunted rooms. For several years Holmes lived in the same street, within a few doors of Fields's house.

At number fifty-four in quaint Pinckney Street, around the corner from Mrs. Fields's and near the former residence of Aldrich, we find the house in which the brilliant George Hilliard lived and died, scarcely changed since the time James Freeman Clarke here married Hawthorne to the lovely Sophia Peabody.

Upon the opposite side, at number eleven, dwells Mrs. E. P. Whipple, widow of the eminent author and critic,—herself a lady of refined critical tastes,—who keeps unchanged the home in which her husband died. In his lifetime a select circle of friends usually assembled here on Sunday evenings,—a circle in which Fields, Bronson Alcott, Lowell, Emerson, Longfellow, Holmes, Sumner, Clarke, Dr. Bartol, Ole Bull, Lucretia Hale, Edwin Booth, and others of similar eminence in letters or art were included. Just around the corner, in Louisburg Square, Bronson Alcott died in the house of his daughter Mrs. Pratt,—the "Meg" of Louisa Alcott's books.

On Beacon Hill, in the next—Mount Vernon—street, we find near the "hub of the Hub" a tall, deep-roomed dwelling, surmounted by an observatory which commands a charming view of the city and its environs, and this is the elegant city home of the poet, novelist, and prince of conversationalists, Thomas Bailey Aldrich. His library, full of treasures, is on a lower floor, but the study in which he pens his delightful compositions is high above the distractions of the world. As one sees the author of "Marjorie Daw" and the recent "Unguarded Gates" among his books, there is no hint of his sixty years in his fresh, ruddy face, with its carefully waxed moustache, nor in his sprightly speech and manner.

In Boston

In the same street, the spacious mansion of ex-Governor Claflin was long a resort of a wise, earnest, and dazzling company of sublimated intellects. This house was in later years the usual haven of Whittier, the gentle Quaker bard, during his visits to Boston; and here, protected by the hostess from the eager kindness of his numerous friends, he spent many restful days when rest was most needed.

Near by, on the same hill-side, the talented authoress of "John Ward, Preacher" inhabits a many-windowed home of sober brick. Within, we find everywhere evidences of the fastidious personality of Mrs. Margaret Deland. In her parlors are dainty articles of furniture and bric-à-brac, wide fireplaces, deep windows full of flowers, many pictures, many more books. In her study and work-room, her desk stands near another fireplace, about it are still more flowers, pictures and books galore; here, not long ago, that tragedy of selfishness—"Philip and His Wife"—was written.

At the sumptuous home of the Sargents in the adjoining street have been held some of the *séances* of the noted Radical Club, in which, as Mrs. Moulton says, "somebody read a paper and everybody else pulled it to pieces." At these sessions such spirits as Emerson, Bronson

In and Out of Literary Boston

Alcott, Holmes, Edward Everett Hale, Carl Schurz, the genial Colonel Higginson, the serene James Freeman Clarke, the mystic Dr. Bartol,—who still lives in retirement in his old home,—and other representatives of advanced thought have discussed the ethics of life as well as of letters.

A plain brick house of three stories in the same quiet street was the abode of Francis Parkman's sister, where, after the death of his wife, the historian spent his winters, his study here being a simple front room on the upper floor, with open fireplace and book-lined walls.

In Park Street, above the Common, the ample mansion of George Ticknor—the chronicler of "Spanish Literature" and the autocrat of literary taste—was during many years a haunt of the best of Boston culture. We find its stately walls still standing, but the interior has been surrendered to the Philistines.

On Beacon Street, but a door or two removed from the birthplace of Wendell Phillips, in a house whose number the poet-lover said he "remembered by thinking of the Thirty-Nine Articles," Longfellow won Miss Appleton to be his wife. Just across the Common, in Carver Street, Hawthorne's son was born.

At many of the homes here mentioned were held the assemblages of the Ladies' Social Club.

In Boston

Among its readers were Agassiz, Emerson, Greene, Whipple, Clarke, and E. E. Hale. It was ironically styled the "Brain Club," and died after many years because, according to one ex-member, "the newer members brought into it too much Supper and Stomach and no Brain at all." A successor has been the Round Table Club, with Colonel Higginson for first president, —its meetings for essays and discussions being held in the homes of its literary or artistic members.

Boston's Belgravia occupies a district which has been reclaimed from the waters of the "Back Bay" of the Charles River,—on whose shore Hawthorne placed the shunned and isolated thatched cottage of Hester Prynne in "The Scarlet Letter," and the windows of many of Boston's Four Hundred overlook the same delightful vista of water, hills, and western skies which to the sad eyes of Hester and little Pearl were a daily vision. On the water side of Beacon Street, within this select region, is the four-floored, picturesque mansion of brick—its front embellished with a growth of ivy which clusters about the bay-windows—where not long ago we found the gentle and genial Holmes sitting among his books, serene in the golden sunset of life, happy in the love of friends and in the benedictions of the thousands his work has uplifted and beatified. The mansion is redolent of literary associations, and throughout its apartments were tastefully disposed articles of virtu, curios, and mementos—literary, artistic, or historic—of affection and regard from Holmes's many friends at home and abroad. His study was a large room at the back of the house, occupying the entire width of the second floor. Its broad window commands a sweep of the Charles, with its tides and its many craft, beyond which the poet could see, as he said, Cambridge where he was born, Harvard where he was educated, and Mount Auburn where he expected to lie in his last sleep. We last saw the "Autocrat" in his easy-chair, among the treasures of this apartment, with a portrait of his ancestress "Dorothy Q" looking down at him from a side wall. His hair was silvered and his kindly face had lost its smoothness,—for he was eighty-five "years young," as he would say,—but his faculties were keen and alert, and, in benign age, his greeting was no less cordial and his outlook upon men and affairs was no less cheery and optimistic than in the flush and vigor of early manhood. In this luxurious study were written several of his twenty-five volumes,—"Over the Teacups" being the most popular of those produced here,

—and we found him still devoting some hours of each day to light literary tasks, oftenest dictating materials for his memoirs, which are yet to be published.

Above the study, and overlooking the river on which he used to row and the farther green hills, is the chamber immortalized in "My Aviary;" and here, as he sat in his favorite chair, surrounded by his family, death came to him, and his spirit peacefully passed into the eternal silence. Then the "Last Leaf" had fallen, to be mourned by all the world.

A door or two from Holmes sometime dwelt the versatile novelist, poet, playwright, and "Altrurian Traveller." A popular print of "Howells in his Library" is an interior of his Beacon Street house; the view of the glassy river-basin, with the roofs and spires of Cambridge rising from banks and bowers of foliage beyond,—which he pictures from the new house of "Silas Lapham" on this street,—is the one Howells daily beheld from his study window here. His latest Boston home was in the same district on the superb Commonwealth Avenue, near the statue of Garrison, and here, in a sumptuous, six-storied, bow-fronted mansion, he wrote "The Shadow of a Dream" and other widely read books.

In and Out of Literary Boston

A modest, old-fashioned house on Beacon Street has long been the home of the poet and starry genius Julia Ward Howe, writer of the "Battle-Hymn of the Republic." Other members of her singularly gifted family have sojourned here, and the "home of the Howes" has been frequented by men and women eminent for culture and thought and for achievement in literature or art.

In the adjacent Marlborough Street recently died the polished author and orator Robert C. Winthrop, and here, too, was the home of Dr. Ellis, the friend of Lowell's father.

Farther away in this newer Boston of luxury and culture is the charming and hospitable home of the poet, essayist, novelist, and critic Mrs. Louise Chandler Moulton, whose American admirers complain that in late years she remains too much in London. When at home, she inhabits a delightful dwelling which, from entrance to attic, teems with pictures, rare books, curios, and other *souvenirs* of her many friends in many lands. In her library, where much of "Garden of Dreams," "Swallow Flights," and other books was written, and where more of all "the work nearest her heart" was accomplished, are preserved many autograph copies of books by recent writers—several of them dedicated to Mrs.

Moulton—and a priceless collection of letters
from illustrious literary workers. In her draw-
ing-rooms one may meet many of the famed
authors of the day,—Higginson, Wendell, Hors-
ford, Bynner, Nora Perry of the charming
books for girls, Miss Conway, Miss Louise Imogen Guiney, Mrs. Howe, Arlo Bates, Adams,
the jocosely serious Robert Grant, and others
of Boston's newer lights of literature.

If we "drive on down Washington Street" with
"Silas Lapham," we shall find in Chester Square
the "Nankeen Square" where he dwelt in his
less ambitious days, and the pretty oval green
with the sturdy trees which the worthy colonel
saw grow from saplings.

In a pleasant dwelling on the contiguous street
lives and works the bright and busy Lucretia P.
Hale, sister of the author-divine. She was the
favorite scholar of Miss Elizabeth Peabody; and
she has, through her writings and her classes,
acquired an influence and discipleship little
smaller than that which Margaret Fuller once
possessed.

Farther south, in the Roxbury district, we
seek the abode of the famed author of "The
Man without a Country." Sauntering along
the shady and delectable Highland Street, we
interrogate a uniformed guardian of the law, who

heartily rejoins, "Dr. Hale's is a temple on the right a block further on: and if any man's fit to live in a temple, it's him." As we walk the "block further on" we think that, however defective his grammar, the policeman's estimate of Hale is beyond criticism and agrees with that of the thousands of readers and friends of the indefatigable author, lecturer, preacher, editor, reformer, and promoter of all good. We find the house—very like a Greek temple—standing back from the street in the midst of an ample lawn, shaded by noble trees and decked with a wealth of shrubbery and bloom. The mansion is a large square edifice, with great dormer-windows in its roofs, surmounted by a cupola, and having in front a lofty portico upheld by heavy Ionic pillars, between which interlacing woodbine forms a leafy screen. Within is a wide hall, and opening out of it are generously proportioned rooms, some of them lined from floor to ceiling with thousands of books. The study is a commodious room, with a "pamphlet-annex" adjoining it on the garden side, and is crammed with book-shelves and drawers, while piles of books, magazines, portfolios, manuscripts, and memoranda are disposed on cases, tables, and stands about the apartment. Everything is obviously arranged for convenient and

ready use, and well it may be so, for this is the
work-room and " thinking-shop" of the hardest-
working literary man in America. The books
which made his first fame were written before
he came to this house; of all the works produced in this study, the numerous poems, romances, histories, essays, editorials, reviews, discussions, translations,—to say nothing of the
many hundreds of well-considered and carefully
written sermons,—we may not here mention
even the names, for no writer since Voltaire is
more fruitful of finished and masterly work. It
is notable that Hale regards " In His Name" as
his best work from a literary point of view; of
his other productions, he thinks some of the
poems of the latest collection, " For Fifty
Years," as good as anything,—"always except-
ing his sermons." Among the abundant treasures of his study, Hale has a most interesting
and valuable collection of autograph letters, of
which he is justly proud. His father was
Nathan Hale of the Boston " Advertiser," his
mother was sister to Edward Everett and herself
an author and translator, his wife is niece to
Mrs. Harriet Beecher Stowe, his son Robert has
already acquired a reputation in the domain of
letters. The doctor himself has been a writer
from childhood, his earliest contributions being

to his father's paper. His illustrious sister declares that in their nursery days she and her brother used to take their meals with the " Advertiser" pinned under their chins,—a practice to which their literary precocity has been attributed. We find Hale at the age of seventy-three blithe and hopeful, working as much and manifestly accomplishing more than ever before.

A little farther out on the same street is the dwelling where William Lloyd Garrison spent his last years, and in this neighborhood lived Mrs. Blake, poet of " Verses Along the Way." Here also are the early home of Miss Guiney and the school to which she was first sent,—or rather " carried neck and heels," because she refused to walk. Close by we find the pleasant home in which Jane G. Austin wrote some of her famed colonial tales and where she died not many months ago; and in the same delightful suburb, a half-mile beyond Hale's house, is the retreat where the beloved author of " Little Women" breathed out her too brief life.

OUT OF BOSTON

I

CAMBRIDGE: ELMWOOD:
MOUNT AUBURN

Holmes's Church-yard—Bridge, Smithy, Chapel, and River of
Longfellow's Verse—Abodes of Lettered Culture—Holmes—
Higginson — Agassiz — Norton — Clough—Howells—Fuller—
Longfellow—Lowell — Longfellow's City of the Dead
and its Precious Graves.

CROSSING the Charles by "The Bridge" of Longfellow's popular poem, a stroll along elm-shaded streets brings us to the ancient Common of Cambridge and a vicinage which has much besides its historic traditions to allure the literary pilgrim. For centuries the site of a celebrated college and a conspicuous centre of learning, it has long been the abiding-place of representatives of the best and foremost in American culture and mental achievement.

Close by the Common, and opposite the remains of the elm beneath which Washington assumed the command of the patriot army, stood the old gambrel-roofed house in which that " gentlest of autocrats," Holmes, was born and reared, and upon whose door-post was first dis-

played his "shingle," on which he whimsically
proposed to inscribe " The Smallest Fevers
Thankfully Received;" across the college grounds
is the home-like edifice where lived the erudite
Professor Felton, loved by Dickens and oft mentioned in his letters; not far away, at the corner
of Broadway, was the home of Agassiz, since
occupied by his son; and a few rods eastward
is the picturesque residence of the witty and
profound Colonel Higginson,—poet, essayist,
novelist, and reformer.   In the adjacent Kirkland Street dwelt the delightful Dr. Estes Howe,
brother-in-law to Lowell, with whom the poet
sometime lived and whom he celebrated as " the
Doctor" in the " Fable for Critics."   Dr. C. C.
Abbott formerly lived in this neighborhood, and
the collections on which his best-known books
are founded are preserved in the near-by Peabody Museum, beyond which we find the tasteful abode of Professor Charles Eliot Norton, the
friend and literary executor of Lowell.   Near
the Common, too, dwelt for a year or so that
rare poet Arthur Clough, author of " The
Bothie" and " Qua Cursum Ventus;" and the
sweet singer Charlotte Fiske Bates—the intimate
friend of Longfellow—had her habitation in the
same neighborhood.   Opposite the southern end
of the Common is the ancient village cemetery

celebrated in the poetry of Holmes and Longfellow; a little way westward, Howells lived
in a delightful rose-embowered cottage and
pleasantly pictured many features of the old
town in the " Charlesbridge" of his " Suburban
Sketches." Two or three furlongs distant,
within the grounds of the Botanic Garden, long
lived the American Linnæus, Professor Asa
Gray.

Of all the Cambridge thoroughfares, the shady
and venerable Brattle Street, which curves westward from the University Press, is most interesting and attractive. Near the Press building
stands the historic Brattle House,—its beautiful
stairway and other antique features preserved by
the Social Club, to whom the property now
belongs,—where Margaret Fuller, the priestess
and queen of modern Transcendentalism, passed
much of her youth and young womanhood, and
where her sister, wife to the poet Ellery Channing, was reared. Margaret, who is said to
have stood for the Theodora of Beaconsfield's
" Lothair," first saw the light in a modest little
dwelling in Main Street nearer the Boston bridge,
and here attended school with Holmes and
Richard Henry Dana; but it was in this Brattle
House that her marvellous, and in some respects
unique, intellectual career commenced. Here

she acquired the moral and mental equipment which fitted her for leadership in the most vital epoch of American culture and thought, and here she attracted and attached all the wisest and noblest spirits within her range. To her here came Theodore Parker, the older Channing, Harriet Martineau, James Freeman Clarke,—the earnest, brilliant, and thoughtful of all ages and conditions. One noble soul who knew her here speaks of her friendship as a "gift of the gods," and some eminent in thought and achievement testify that they have ever striven toward standards set up for them by her in that early period of her residence here.

Close by Miss Fuller's home, "under a spreading chestnut-tree" at the intersection of Story Street, stood the smithy of Pratt, who was immortalized by Longfellow as "The Village Blacksmith." To the poet, passing daily on the way between his home and the college, the "mighty man" at his anvil in the shaded smithy was long a familiar vision. The tree—a horse-chestnut—has been removed, the shop has given place to a modern dwelling, and years ago the worthy smith rejoined his wife, "singing in Paradise."

A few steps westward from the site of the smithy is the "Chapel of St. John" of another sweet poem of Longfellow; and just beyond this we find, bowered by lilacs and environed by acres of shade and sward, the colonial Cragie House, once the sojourn of Washington, but holding for us more precious associations, since Sparks, Worcester, and Everett have lived within its time-honored walls, and our popular poet of grace and sentiment for near half a century here had his home, and from here passed into the unknown. The picturesque mansion wears the aspect of an old acquaintance, and the interior, with its princely proportioned rooms, spacious fireplaces, wide halls, curious carvings and tiles, has much that Longfellow has shared with his readers. On the entrance door is the ponderous knocker; a landing of the broad stairway holds "The Old Clock on the Stairs;" at the right of the hall is the study, with its priceless mementos of the tender and sympathetic bard who wrought here the most and best of his life-work, from early manhood onward into the mellow twilight of sweet and benign age. Here is his chair, vacated by him but a few days before he died; his desk; his inkstand which had been Coleridge's; his pen with its "link from the chain of Bonnivard;" the antique pitcher of his "Drinking Song;" the fireplace of "The Wind over the Chimney;" the arm-chair carved from the "spreading chestnut-tree" of the smithy, which was presented to him by the village children and celebrated in his poem "From my Arm-Chair." About us here are his cherished books, his pictures, his manuscripts, all his precious belongings, and from his window we see, beyond the Longfellow Memorial Park, the river so often sung in his verse, "stealing onward, like the stream of life." In this room Washington held his war councils. Of the many intellectual *séances* its walls have witnessed we contemplate with greatest pleasure the Wednesday evening meetings of the "Dante Club," when Lowell, Howells, Fields, Norton, Greene, and other friends and scholars sat here with Longfellow to revise the new translation of Dante.

The book-lined apartment over the study—once the bedchamber of Washington and later of Talleyrand—was occupied by Longfellow when he first lived as a lodger in the old house. It was here he heard "Footsteps of Angels" and "Voices of the Night," and saw by the fitful firelight the "Being Beauteous" at his side; here he wrote "Hyperion" and the earlier poems which made him known and loved in every clime. Later this room became the nursery of his children, and some of the grotesque

tiles which adorn its chimney are mentioned in his poem " To a Child :"

> " The lady with the gay macaw,
>   The dancing-girl, the grave bashaw,
>   The Chinese mandarin."

Along the western façade of the mansion stretches a wide veranda, where the poet was wont to take his daily exercise when " the goddess Neuralgia" or " the two Ws" (Work and Weather) prevented his walking abroad. In this stately old house his children w?re born and reared, here his wife met her tragic death, and here his daughter—the " grave Alice" of " The Children's Hour"—abides and preserves its precious relics, while " laughing Allegra" (Anna) and " Edith with golden hair"—now Mrs. Dana and Mrs. Thorp—have dwellings within the grounds of their childhood home, and their brother Ernst owns a modern cottage a few rods westward on the same street.

In Sparks Street, just out of Brattle, dwelt the author Robert Carter,—familiarly, " The Don,"—sometime secretary to Prescott and long the especial friend of Lowell, with whom he was associated in the editorship of the short-lived " Pioneer." Carter's home here was the rendezvous of a circle of choice spirits, where one might often meet " Prince" Lowell,—as his friends delighted to call him,—Bartlett of " Familiar Quotations," and that " songless poet" John Holmes, brother of the " American Montaigne."

A short walk under the arching elms of Brattle Street brings us to Elmwood, the life-long home of Lowell. The house, erected by the last British lieutenant-governor of the province, is a plain, square structure of wood, three stories in height, and is surrounded by a park of simple and natural beauty, whose abundant growth of trees gives to some portions of the grounds the sombreness and apparent seclusion of a forest. A gigantic hedge of trees encloses the place like a leafy wall, excluding the vision of the world and harboring thousands of birds who tenant its shades. Some of the aquatic fowl of the vicinage are referred to in Longfellow's " Herons of Elmwood." In the old mansion, long the home of Elbridge Gerry, Lowell was born and grew to manhood, and to it he brought the bride of his youth, the lovely Maria White, herself the writer of some exquisite poems; here, a few years later, she died in the same night that a child was born to Longfellow, whose poem " The Two Angels" commemorates both events. Here, too, Lowell lost his children one by one

until a daughter, the present Mrs. Burnett,—
now owner and occupant of Elmwood,—alone
remained. During the poet's stay abroad, his
house was tenanted by Mrs. Ole Bull and by
Lowell's brother-bard Bailey Aldrich, who in
this sweet retirement wrought some of his delicious work. To the beloved trees and birds
of his old home Lowell returned from his em-
bassage, and here, with his daughter, he passed
his last years among his books and a chosen circle of friends. Here, where he wished to die, he
died, and here his daughter preserves his former
home and its contents unchanged since he was
borne hence to his burial. Until the death of
his father, Lowell's study was an upper front
room at the left of the entrance. It is a plain,
low-studded corner apartment, which the poet
called "his garret," and where he slept as a boy.
Its windows now look only into the neighboring
trees, but when autumn has shorn the boughs of
their foliage the front window commands a wide
level of the sluggish Charles and its bordering
lowlands, while the side window overlooks the
beautiful slopes of Mount Auburn, where Lowell
now lies with his poet-wife and the children
who went before. His study windows suggested
the title of his most interesting volume of prose
essays. In this upper chamber he wrote his

"Conversations on the Poets" and the early poems which made his fame,—"Irene," "Prometheus," "Rhœcus," "Sir Launfal,"—which was composed in five days,—and the first series of that collection of grotesque drolleries, "The Biglow Papers." Here also he prepared his editorial contributions to the "Atlantic." His later study was on the lower floor, at the left of the ample hall which traverses the centre of the house. It is a prim and delightful old-fashioned apartment, with low walls, a wide and cheerful fireplace, and pleasant windows which look out among the trees and lilacs upon a long reach of lawn. In this room the poet's best-loved books, copiously annotated by his hand, remain upon his shelves; here we see his table, his accustomed chair, the desk upon which he wrote the "Commemoration Ode," "Under the Willows," and many famous poems, besides the volumes of prose essays. In this study he sometimes gathered his classes in Dante, and to him here came his friends familiarly and informally,—for "receptions" were rare at Elmwood: most often came "The Don," "The Doctor," Norton, Owen, Bartlett, Felton, Stillman,—less frequently Godkin, Fields, Holmes, Child, Motley, Edmund Quincy, and the historian Parkman.

Mount Auburn

While the older trees of the place were planted by Gerry, the pines and clustering lilacs were rooted by Lowell or his father. All who remember the poet's passionate love for this home will rejoice in the assurance that the old mansion, with its precious associations and mementos, and the acres immediately adjoining it, will not be in any way disturbed during the life of his daughter and her children. At most, the memorial park which has been planned by the literary people of Boston and Cambridge will include only that portion of the grounds which belonged to the poet's brothers and sisters.

A narrow street separates the hedges of Elmwood from the peaceful shades of Mount Auburn, —the " City of the Dead" of Longfellow's sonnet. Lowell thought this the most delightful spot on earth. The late Francis Parkman told the writer that Lowell, in his youth, had confided to him that he habitually went into the cemetery at midnight and sat upon a tombstone, hoping to find there the poetic afflatus. He confessed he had not succeeded, and was warned by his friend that the custom would bring him more rheumatism than inspiration. Dr. Ellis testified that at this period his friend Dr. Lowell often expressed to him his anxiety " lest his son

James would amount to nothing, because he had taken to writing poetry."

In the sanctuary of Mount Auburn we find many of the names mentioned in these chapters, —names written on the scroll of fame, blazoned on title-pages, borne in the hearts of thousands of readers in all lands,—now, alas! inscribed above their graves. From the eminence of Mount Auburn, we look upon Longfellow's river "stealing with silent pace" around the sacred enclosure; the verdant meads along the stream; the distant cities, erst the abodes of those who sleep about us here,—for whom life's fever is ended and life's work done. Near this summit, Charlotte Cushman rests at the base of a tall obelisk, her favorite myrtle growing dense and dark above her. By the elevated Ridge Path, on a site long ago selected by him, Longfellow lies in a grave decked with profuse flowers and marked by a monument of brown stone. On Fountain Avenue we find a beautiful spot, shaded by two giant trees, which was a beloved resort of Lowell, and where he now lies among his kindred, his sepulchre marked by a simple slab of slate: "Good-night, sweet Prince!" Not far away is the beautiful Jackson plot, where not long ago the beloved Holmes was tenderly laid in the same grave with his wife beneath a burden of flowers. Some of the blossoms we lately saw upon this grave were newly placed by the creator of " Micah Clarke" and " Sherlock Holmes," Dr. Conan Doyle. By a great oak near the main avenue is the sarcophagus of Sumner, and one shady slope bears the memorial of Margaret Fuller and her husband,—buried beneath the sea on the coast of Fire Island. Near by we find the grave of " Fanny Fern,"— wife of Parton and sister of N. P. Willis,—with its white cross adorned with exquisitely carved ferns; the pillar of granite and marble which designates the resting-place of Everett; the granite boulder—its unchiselled surface overgrown with the lichens he loved—which covers the ashes of Agassiz; the simple sarcophagus of Rufus Choate; the cenotaph of Kirkland; the tomb of Spurzheim; and on the lovely slopes about us, under the dreaming trees, amid myriad witcheries of bough and bloom, are the enduring memorials of affection beneath which repose the mortal parts of Sargent, Quincy, Story, Parker, Worcester, Greene, Bigelow, William Ellery Channing, Edwin Booth, Phillips Brooks, and many like them whom the world will not soon forget.

In this sweet summer day, their place of rest is so quiet and beautiful,—with the birds singing here their lowest and tenderest songs, the soft winds breathing a lullaby in the leafy boughs, the air full of a grateful peace and calm, the trees spreading their great branches in perpetual benediction above the turf-grown graves,—it seems that here, if anywhere, the restless wayfarer might learn to love restful death.

OUT OF BOSTON

II

BELMONT: THE WAYSIDE INN: HOME OF WHITTIER

A FEW miles westward from the classic shades of Cambridge we found, perched upon a breezy height of Belmont, a picturesque, red-roofed villa, for some years the summer home of our " Altrurian Traveller." From its verandas he overlooked a slumberous plain, diversified with meads, fields, country-seats, and heavy-tinted copses, and bordered by a circle of verdant hills; while on the eastern horizon rises the distant city, crowned by the resplendent dome of the capitol. In his dainty white study here, with its gladsome fireplace and curious carvings and mottoes, Howells wrote—besides other good things—his " Lady of the Aroostook," in which some claim to have discerned an answer to Henry James's " Daisy Miller."

In and Out of Literary Boston

In this neighborhood is the valley of " Beaver Brook," a favorite haunt of Lowell, to which he brought the English poet Arthur Clough. The old mill is removed, but we find the waterfall and the other romantic features little changed since the poet depicted the ideal beauties of this dale, in what has been adjudged one of the most artistic poems of modern times.

In a charming retreat among the hills of Arlington, scarce a mile away from Howells's sometime Belmont home, dwells and writes that genial and gifted poet and novelist, John T. Trowbridge, whose books — notably his war-time tales—have found readers round the world.

Westward again from Belmont, a prolonged drive through a delightful country brings us to "Sudbury town" and the former hostelry of 'Squire Howe,—the " Wayside Inn" of Longfellow's " Tales." Our companion and guide is one who well knew the old house and its neighborhood in the halcyon days when Professor Treadwell, Parsons,—the poet of the " Bust of Dante,"—and the quiet coterie of Longfellow's friends came, summer after summer, to find rest and seclusion under its ample roof and sheltering trees, among the hills of this remote region. The environment of fragrant meadow and smiling field, of deep wood glade and forest-clad height, is indeed alluring. About the ancient inn remain some of the giant elms and the "oak-trees, broad and high," shading it now as in the day when the "Tales" immortalized it with the "Tabard" of Chaucer; while through the near meadow circles the "well-remembered brook" of the poet's verse, in which his friends saw the inverted landscape and their own faces "looking up at them from below."

The house is a great, old-fashioned, bare and weather-worn edifice of wood,—"somewhat fallen to decay."—standing close upon the highway. Its two stories of spacious rooms are supplemented by smaller chambers in a vast attic; two or three chimneys, "huge and tiled and tall," rise through its gambrel roofs among the bowering foliage; a wing abuts upon one side and imparts a pleasing irregularity to the otherwise plain parallelogram. The wide, low-studded rooms are lighted by windows of many small panes. Among the apartments we find the one once occupied by Major Molineaux, "whom Hawthorne hath immortal made," and that of Dr. Parsons, the laureate of this place, who has celebrated it in the stanzas of "Old House at Sudbury" and other poems. But it is the old inn parlor which most interests the literary visitor,—a great, low, square apartment, with oaken floors, ponderous beams overhead, and a broad hearth, where in the olden time blazed a log fire whose ruddy glow filled the room and shone out through the windows. It is this room which Longfellow peoples with his friends, who sat about the old fireplace and told his "Tales of a Wayside Inn." The "rapt musician" whose transfiguring portraiture we have in the Prelude is Ole Bull; the student "of old books and days" is Henry Wales; the young Sicilian, "in sight of Etna born and bred," is Luigi Monti, who dined every Sunday with Longfellow; the "Spanish Jew from Alicant" is Edrelei, a Boston Oriental dealer; the "Theologian from the school of Cambridge on the Charles" is Professor Daniel Treadwell; the Poet is T. W. Parsons, the Dantean student and translator of "Divina Commedia;" the Landlord is 'Squire Lyman Howe, the portly bachelor who then kept this "Red Horse Tavern," as it was called. Most of this goodly circle have been here in the flesh, and our companion has seen them in this old room, as well as Longfellow himself, who came here years afterward, when the Landlord was dead and the poet's company had left the old inn forever.

In this room we see the corner where stood the ancient spinet, the spot on the wall where hung the highly colored coat of arms of Howe and the sword of his knightly grandfather near Queen Mary's pictured face, the places on the prismatic-hued windows where the names of Molineaux, Treadwell, etc., had been inscribed by hands that now are dust.

Descendants of the woman who died of the "Shoc o' Num Palsy" are said to live in the neighborhood, as well as some other odd characters who are embalmed in Parsons's humorous verse. But the ancient edifice is no longer an inn; the Red Horse on the swinging sign-board years ago ceased to invite the weary wayfarer to rest and cakes and ale; the memory-haunted chambers, where starry spirits met and tarried in the golden past, were later inhabited by laborers, who displayed the rooms for a fee and plied the pilgrim with lies anent the former famed occupants. The storied structure has recently passed to the possession of appreciative owners,—Hon. Herbert Howe being one of them,—who have made the repairs needful for its preservation and have placed it in the charge of a proper custodian.

A longer way out of Boston, in another direction, our guest is among the haunts of the beloved Quaker bard. On the bank of the Merrimac—his own "lowland river"—and among darkly wooded hills of hackmatack and pine, we find the humble farm-house, guarded by giant sentinel poplars, where eighty-eight years agone Whittier came into the world.

Among the plain and bare apartments, with their low ceilings, antique cross-beams, and multipaned windows, we see the lowly chamber of his birth; the simple study where his literary work was begun; the great kitchen, with its brick oven and its heavy crane in the wide fireplace, where he laid the famous winter's evening scene in "Snow-Bound," peopling the plain "old rude-furnished room" with the persons he here best knew and loved. We see the dwelling little changed since the time when Whittier dwelt—a dark-haired lad—under its roof; it is now carefully preserved, and through the old rooms are disposed articles of furniture from his Amesbury cottage, which are objects of interest to many visitors.

All about the place are spots of tender identification of poet and poem: here are the brook and the garden wall of his "Barefoot Boy;" the scene of his "Telling the Bees;" the spring and meadow of "Maud Muller;" not far away, with the sumachs and blackberries clustering about

it still, is the site of the rude academy of his
"School Days;" and beyond the low hill the
grasses grow upon the grave of the dear, brown-
eyed girl who "hated to go above him." We
may still loiter beneath the overarching syca-
mores planted by poor Tallant,—"pioneer of
Erin's outcasts,"—where young Whittier pondered the story of "Floyd Ireson with the hard
heart."

Delightful rambles through the country-side
bring us to many scenes familiar to the tender
poet and by him made familiar to all the world.
Thus we come to the "stranded village" of
Aunt Mose,—"the muttering witch-wife of the
gossip's tale,"—where Whittier found the materials out of which he wrought the touching
poem "The Countess," and where we see the
poor low rooms in which pretty, blue-eyed
Mary Ingalls was born and lived a too brief
life of love, and her sepulchre—now reclaimed
from a tangle of brake and brier—in the lonely
old burial-ground that "slopes against the
west." Her grave is in the row nearest the
dusty highway, and is marked by a mossy
slab of slate, which is now protected from
the avidity of relic-gatherers by a net-work of
iron, bearing the inscription, "The Grave of
the Countess."

Thus, too, we come to the ruined foundation of the cottage of " Mabel Martin, the Witch's Daughter," and look thence upon other haunts of the beloved bard, as well as upon his river " glassing the heavens" and the wave-like swells of foliage-clad hills which are " The Laurels" of his verse. In West Newbury, the town of his " Northman's Written Rock," we find the comfortable " Maplewood" homestead where lived and lately died the supposed sweetheart of the poet's early manhood.

Whittier's beloved Amesbury, the " home of his heart," is larger and busier than he knew it, but, as we dally on its dusty avenues, we find them aglow with living memories of the sweet singer. In Friend Street stands—still occupied by Whittier's former friends—the plain little frame house which was so long his home. A bay window has been placed above the porch, but the place is otherwise little changed since he left it; the same noble elms shade the front, the fruit-trees he planted and pruned and beneath which the saddened throng sat at his funeral are in the garden; here too are the grape-vines which were the especial objects of his loving care,—one of them grown from a rootlet sent to him in a letter by Charles Sumner.

Whittier's Amesbury Cottage

Within, we see the famous "garden room," which was his sanctum and workshop, and where this gentle man of peace waged valiant warfare with his pen for the rights of man. In this room, with its sunny outlook among his vines and pear-trees, he kept his chosen books, his treasured souvenirs; and here he welcomed his friends,— Longfellow, Fields, Sumner, Lowell, Colonel Higginson, Bayard Taylor, Mrs. Thaxter, Mrs. Phelps-Ward, Alice Cary, Lucy Larcom, Sarah Orne Jewett, and many another illustrious child of genius.

A quaint Franklin fireplace stood by one side wall,—usually surmounted in summer by a bouquet; in the nook between this and the sash-door was placed an old-fashioned writing-desk, and here he wrote many of the poems which brought him world-wide fame and voiced the convictions and the conscience of half the nation. Here are still preserved some of his cherished books. Above the study was Whittier's bedchamber, near the rooms of his mother, his "youngest and dearest" sister, and the "dear aunt" (Mercy) of "Snow-Bound," who came with him to this home and shared it until their deaths. After the others were gone, the brother and sister long dwelt here alone, later a niece was for some years his house-keeper, and at her marriage the poet gave up most of the house to some old friends, who kept his study and chamber in constant readiness for his return upon the prolonged sojourns which were continued until his last year of life,—this being always his best-loved home.

Near by are the " painted shingly town-house" of his verse, where during many years he failed not to meet with his neighbors to deposit " the freeman's vote for Freedom," and the little, wooden Friends' meeting-house, where he loved to sit in silent introspection among the people of his faith. The trees which now shade its plain old walls with abundant foliage were long ago planted by his hands. The " Powow Hill" of his " Preacher" and " 'The Prophecy of Samuel Sewall" rises steeply near his home, and was a favorite resort, to which he often came, alone or with his guests. One who has often stood with Whittier there pilots us to his accustomed place on the lofty rounded summit, whence we overlook the village, the long reach of the " sea-seeking" river, and the entrancing scene pictured by the poet in the beautiful lines of " Miriam."

From these precious haunts our pilgrim shoon trace the revered bard to the peaceful precincts

Whittier's Tomb

of the God's-acre—just without the town—
where, in a sequestered spot beneath a dark cedar
which sobs and soughs in the summer wind, his
mortal part is forever laid, with his beloved
sister and kindred, within

" the low green tent
Whose curtain never outward swings."

OUT OF BOSTON

III

SALEM: WHITTIER'S OAK-KNOLL AND BEYOND

Cemetery of Hawthorne's Ancestors–Birthplace of Hawthorne and his Wife–Where Fame was won–House of the Seven Gables–Custom-House–Where Scarlet Letter was written –Main Street and Witch Hill – Sights from a Steeple– Later Home of Whittier–Norman's Woe–Lucy Larcom– Parton, etc.–Rivermouth–Thaxter.

A HALF-HOUR'S jaunt by train brings us to the shaded streets of quaint old Salem and the scenes of Hawthorne's early life, work, and triumph. Here we find on Charter Street, in the old cemetery of " Dr. Grimshaw's Secret" and " Dolliver Romance," the sunken and turf-grown graves of Hawthorne's mariner ancestors, some of whom sailed forth on the ocean of eternity nearly two centuries ago. Among the curiously carved gravestones of slate we see that of John Hathorn, the " witch-judge" of Haw-thorne's " Note-Books." Close at hand repose the ancestors of the novelist's wife, and the Doctor Swinnerton who preceded " Dolliver" and who was called to consider the cause of

Colonel Pyncheon's death in the opening chapter of "The House of the Seven Gables."

The sombre house which encroaches upon a corner of the cemetery enclosure—with the green billows surging about it so closely that its side windows are within our reach from the gravestones—was the home of the Peabodys, whence Hawthorne wooed the amiable Sophia, and where, in his tales, he domiciled Grandsir "Dolliver" and also "Doctor Grimshaw" with Ned and Elsie. We found it a rather depressing, hip-roofed, low-studded, and irregular edifice of wood, standing close upon the street, and obviously degenerated a little from the degree of respectability—"not sinking below the boundary of the genteel"—which the romancer ascribed to it. The little porch or hood protects the front entrance, and the back door communicates with the cemetery,—a circumstance which recalls the novelist's fancy that the dead might get out of their graves at night and steal into this house to warm themselves at the convenient fireside.

Not many rods distant, in Union Street, stands the little house where Captain Hathorn left his family when he went away to sea, and where the novelist was born. The street is small, shabby, shadeless, dispiriting,—its inhabitants not select.

The house—builded by Hawthorne's grandfather and lately numbered twenty-seven — stands close to the sidewalk, upon which its door-stone encroaches, leaving no space for flower or vine; the garden where Hawthorne "rolled on a grass-plot under an apple-tree and picked abundant currants" is despoiled of turf and tree, and the wooden house walls rise bare and bleak. It is a plain, uninviting, eight-roomed structure, with a lower addition at the back, and with a square central chimney-stack rising like a tower above the gambrel roof. The rooms are low and contracted, with quaint corner fireplaces and curiously designed closets, and with protuberant beams crossing the ceilings. From the entrance between the front rooms a narrow winding stair leads to an upper landing, at the left of which we find the little, low-ceiled chamber where, ninety years ago, America's greatest romancer first saw the light. It is one of the most cheerless of rooms, with rude fireplace of bricks, a mantel of painted planks, and two small windows which look into the verdureless yard. In a modest brick house upon the opposite side of the street, and but a few rods distant from the birthplace of her future husband, Hawthorne's wife was born five years subsequent to his nativity.

The Manning House

Abutting upon the back yard of Hawthorne's birthplace is the old Manning homestead of his maternal ancestors, the home of his own youth and middle age and the theatre of his struggles and triumph. It is known as number twelve Herbert Street, and is a tall, unsightly, erratic fabric of wood, with nothing pleasing or gracious in its aspect or environment. The ugly and commonplace character of his surroundings here during half his life must have been peculiarly depressing to such a sensitive temperament as Hawthorne's, and doubtless accounts for his mental habits. That he had no joyous memories of this old house his letters and journals abundantly show. Its interior arrangement has been somewhat changed to accommodate the several families of laborers who have since inhabited it, and one front room seems to have been used as a shop; but it is not difficult to identify the haunted chamber which was Hawthorne's bedroom and study. This little, dark, dreary apartment under the eaves, with its multipaned window looking down into the room where he was born, is to us one of the most interesting of all the Hawthorne shrines. Here the magician kept his solitary vigil during the long period of his literary probation, shunning his family, declining all human sympathy and fellowship, for some time going abroad only after nightfall; here he studied, pondered, wrote, revised, destroyed, day after day as the slow months went by; and here, after ten years of working and waiting for the world to know him, he triumphantly recorded, " In this dismal chamber FAME was won." Here he wrote " Twice-Told Tales" and many others, which were published in various periodicals, and here, after his residence at the old Manse,—for it was to this Manning house that he " always came back, like the bad halfpenny," as he said,—he completed the "Mosses." This old dwelling is one of the several which have been fixed upon as being the original " House of the Seven Gables," despite the novelist's averment that the Pyncheon mansion was " of materials long in use for constructing castles in the air." The pilgrim in Salem will be persistently assured that a house which stands near the shore by the foot of Turner Street, and is known as number thirty-four, was the model of Hawthorne's structure. It is an antique edifice of some architectural pretensions, displays five fine gables, and has spacious wainscoted and frescoed apartments, with quaint mantels and other evidences of colonial stateliness. It was an object familiar to the novelist from his boyhood,—he had often visited it while it was the home of pretty "Susie" Ingersol,—and it may have suggested the style of architecture he employed for the visionary mansion of the tale. The names Maule and Pyncheon, employed in the story, were those of old residents of Salem.

But a few rods from Herbert Street is the Custom-House where Hawthorne did irksome duty as "Locofoco Surveyor," its exterior being —except for the addition of a cupola—essentially unchanged since his description was written, and its interior being even more somnolent than of yore. The wide and worn granite steps still lead up to the entrance portico; above it hovers the same enormous specimen of the American eagle, and a recent reburnishing has rendered even more evident the truculent attitude of that "unhappy fowl." The entry-way where the venerable officials of Hawthorne's time sat at the receipt of customs has been renovated, the antique chairs in which they used to drowse, "tilted back against the wall," have given place to others of more modern and elegant fashion, and the patriarchal dozers themselves—lying now in the profounder slumber of death—are replaced by younger and sprightlier successors, who wear their dignities and pocket their emoluments. At the left we find the room, "fifteen feet square and of lofty height," which was Hawthorne's office during the period of his surveyorship: it is no longer "cobwebbed and dingy," but is tastefully refitted and refurnished, and the once sanded floor, which the romancer "paced from corner to corner" like a caged lion, is now neatly carpeted. The "exceedingly decrepit and infirm" chairs, and the three-legged stool on which he lounged with his elbow on the old pine desk, have been retired, and the desk itself is now tenderly cherished among the treasures of the Essex Institute, on Essex Street, a few blocks distant, where the custodian proudly shows us the name of Hawthorne graven within the lid, in some idle moment, by the thumb-nail of the novelist. Some yellow documents bearing his official stamp and signature are preserved at the Custom-House, and the courteous official who now occupies Hawthorne's room displays to us here a rough stencil plate marked "Salem N Hawthorne Surr 1847," by means of which knowledge of Hawthorne's existence was blazoned abroad "on pepper-bags, cigar-boxes, and bales of dutiable merchandise," instead of on title-pages. The arched window, by which stood his desk, commands a view upon which his vision often rested, and which seems to us decidedly more pleasing and attractive than he has led us to expect. The picturesque old wharf in the foreground, the white-sailed shipping, and a shimmering expanse of water extending to the farther bold headlands of the coast form, we think, a pleasant picture for the lounger here.

The apartment opposite to Hawthorne's was, in his day, occupied by the brave warrior General James Miller, who is graphically described as the "old Collector" in the introduction to "Scarlet Letter;" in the room directly above it —which is the private office of the present chief executive, the genial Collector Waters— a portrait of the hero of Lundy's Lane now looks down from the wall upon the visitor; but no picture of Hawthorne is to be found in the edifice.

An ample room at the right of the hall on the second floor, now handsomely fitted and furnished, was in Hawthorne's time open and unfinished, its bare beams festooned with cobwebs and its floor lumbered with barrels and bundles of musty official documents; and it was here that he discovered, among the accumulated rubbish of the past, the " scarlet, gold-embroidered letter," and the manuscript of Surveyor Prue,—Hawthorne's ancient predecessor in office,—which recorded the "doings and sufferings" of Hester Prynne.

A short walk from the Custom-House brings us to the spot where, with "public notices posted upon its front and an iron goblet chained to its waist," stood that "eloquent monologist," the town-pump of Hawthorne's famous "Rill." Already its locality, at the corner of Essex and Washington Streets, is pointed out with pride as being among the sites memorable in the town's history, and thus the playful prophecy with which Hawthorne terminates the sketch of his official life is more than fulfilled.

The spacious and well-preserved old frame house at number fourteen Mall Street—a neighborhood superior to that of his former residences—was Hawthorne's abode for three or four years. It was here that he, on the day of his official death, announced to his wife, "Well, Sophie, my head is off, so I must write a book;" and here, in the ensuing six months, disturbed and distressed by illness of his family, by the death of his mother, and by financial needs, he wrote our most famous romance, "The Scarlet Letter." A bare little room in the front of the third story was his study here, and while he wrote in solitude his wife worked in a sitting-room just beneath, decorating lamp-shades whose sale helped to sustain the household.

As we saunter along the " Main Street" of Hawthorne's sketch and the other shady avenues he knew so well, the curious old town, which in his discontent he called tame and unattractive, seems to our eyes picturesque and beautiful, with its wide elm-bordered streets, its grassy way-sides, its many gardens and square, embowered dwellings, not greatly changed since he knew them. If we follow " the long and lazy street" to the Witch Hill, which the novelist describes in " Alice Doane's Appeal," we may behold from that unhappy spot, where men and women suffered death for imagined misdoing, the whole of Hawthorne's Salem, with the environment he pictures in " Sights from a Steeple." We see the house-roofs of the town—half hidden by clustering foliage—extending now from the slopes of the fateful hill to the glinting waters of the harbor; the farther expanse of field and meadow, dotted with white villages and scored with shadowy water-ways; the craggy coast, with the Atlantic thundering endlessly against its headlands. Yonder is the steeple of Haw-thorne's vision, beyond is the scene of the ex-quisite " Footprints in the Sand," and across the blue of the rippling sea we behold the place of the fierce fight in which the gallant Lawrence lost at once his ship and his life.

Not far from Salem is Oak-Knoll, where the white-souled Whittier, "wearing his silver crown," passed "life's late afternoon" with his devoted relatives. It is a delightful, sheltered old country-seat, with wide lawns, and scores of broad acres wooded with noble trees, beneath which the poet loved to stroll or sit, soothed and inspirited by the gracious and generous beauty of the scene about him.

One spot in the glimmering shade of an over-arching oak is shown as his favorite resort. Close by the house is a circular, green-walled garden, where, in summer mornings, he delighted to work with rake and hoe among the flowers. The mansion is a dreamful, old-fashioned edifice, with wide and lofty piazzas, whose roofs are upheld by massive columns; and, with its grand setting of trees, it presents a pleasing picture. Whittier's study—a pleasant, cheerful room, with a delightful outlook and sunny exposure, a friendly-looking fireplace, and a glass door open-ing upon the veranda—was especially erected for him in a corner of the house, and here his later poems were penned. A bright and ample chamber above the parlor was his sleeping-apart-ment.

Whittier—Longfellow, etc.

The sweet poetess Miss Preston and the sprightly and versatile "Gail Hamilton" dwelt in the neighborhood and came often to this room to talk with the "transplanted prophet of Amesbury." Lucy Larcom and that "Sappho of the isles," Celia Thaxter, came less frequently. The place is still occupied by the relatives Whittier loved, who have preserved essentially unchanged the scenes he here inhabited.

A little farther up the rock-bound coast are the scene of Lucy Larcom's touching poem "Hannah's at the Window Binding Shoes;" the hearth-stone where Longfellow saw his "Fire of Drift-Wood;" and the bleak sea-side home of "Floyd Ireson" of Whittier's verse. Beyond these lie the sometime summer homes of the poet Dana, Harriet Prescott Spofford, Fields, and Whipple, with that Mecca of the tourist, the savage reef of Norman's Woe,—celebrated in Longfellow's pathetic poem as the scene of "The Wreck of the Hesperus,"—not far away; while across the harbor a summer resort of the gifted Elizabeth Stuart Phelps Ward stands—an "Old Maid's Paradise" no longer—among the rocks of the shore.

By the mouth of Whittier's "lowland river" we find the birthplace of Lloyd Garrison, the ancestral abode of the Longfellows, the tomb of Whitefield beneath the spot where he preached, the once sojourn of Talleyrand. Here, too, still inhabited by his family, we find the large, three-storied corner house in which Parton spent his last twenty years of busy life, and the low book-lined attic study where, in his cherished easy-chair with his manuscript resting upon a lap-board, he did much of his valuable work.

Still farther northward, we come to the ancient town of Aldrich's " Bad Boy"-hood,—immortalized as the "Rivermouth" of his prose,— the place of Longfellow's " Lady Wentworth," the home of Hawthorne's Sir William Pepperell ; and to the picturesque island realm of that " Princess of Thule," Celia Thaxter, and her gifted poet-brother Laighton ;—but these shrines are worthy of a separate pilgrimage.

OUT OF BOSTON

IV

WEBSTER'S MARSHFIELD: BROOK FARM, ETC

Scenes of the Old Oaken Bucket—Webster's Home and Grave—Where Emerson won his Wife — Home of Miss Peabody — Parkman — Miss Guiney — Aldrich's Ponkapog — Farm of Ripley's Community — Relics and Reminiscences.

ONE day's excursion out of Boston is southward through the birthplace and ancestral home of the brilliant essayist Quincy to the boyhood haunts of Woodworth and the scenes which inspired his sweetest lyric. In Scituate, by the village of Greenbush, we find the well of the "Old Oaken Bucket" remaining at the site of the dwelling where the poet was born and reared. Most of the "loved scenes" of his childhood—the wide-spreading pond, the venerable orchard, the flower-decked meadow, the "deep-tangled wildwood"—may still be seen, little changed since he knew them; but the rock of the cataract has been removed and the cascade itself somewhat altered by the widening of the highway; the "cot of his father" has given place to a modern farm-house; and the "moss-covered bucket that hung in the well" has been supplanted by a convenient but unpoetical pump.

A few miles beyond this romantic spot we come to the Marshfield home of Daniel Webster, set in the midst of a pleasant rural region, not far from the ancient abode of Governor Winslow of the Plymouth colony. On the site of Webster's farm-house of thirty rooms— destroyed by fire some years ago—his son's widow erected a pretty and tasteful modern cottage, in which she preserved many relics of the illustrious statesman and orator, which had been rescued from the flames. Some of the relics were afterward removed to Boston, and, the family becoming extinct with the death of Mrs. Fletcher Webster, the place found an appreciatory proprietor in Mr. Walton Hall, a Boston business-man who was reared in this neighborhood, where Webster's was "a name to conjure by."

The objects connected with the memory of the statesman have been as far as possible preserved, and we find the cottage partially furnished with his former belongings. Here we see his writing-table, covered with ink-stained green baize; his phenomenally large arm-chair with seat of leather; the andirons from his study fireplace; the heavy cane he used in his walks

about the farm; portraits of the great *genius loci*
—one of them representing him in his coarse
farm attire—and of members of his family; a
fine cabinet of beetles and butterflies presented
to him by the Emperor of Brazil; and a number
of paintings, articles of furniture, and bric-à-brac
which had once been Webster's.

Near the house stand the great memorial elms,
each planted by Webster's hand at the death of
one of his children. His favorite tree, beneath
which his coffined figure lay at his funeral, was
injured by the fire and has since been removed.
Behind the house is a pretty lakelet, on whose
surface—by his desire—lights were kept burning at night during his last illness, so that he
might see them from his bed in the Pink Room
where he died.

His study window looked out through a colonnade of trees upon the hill-side cemetery—a
furlong distant—where he now sleeps in a spot
he loved and chose for his sepulchre. His
tomb, on the brow of the hill, is marked by a
huge mound of earth crowned by a ponderous
marble slab. The memorial stones about it
were erected by him to commemorate his
family, already sleeping in the vault here before
he came to lie among them:—all save one, and
that one died at Bull Run.

In and Out of Literary Boston

Not far away lie Governor Winslow and the Peregrine White who was born on the Mayflower. From among the neglected graves we look abroad upon the acres Webster tilled, the creeks he fished, the meadows he hunted, the haunts of his leisure during many years: on the one hand, we see a stretch of verdant pastures and lowly hills dotted by white cottages and bounded by distant forests; on the other hand, across the wave-like dunes and glistening sands we see a silver rim flecked with white sails,—the ocean, whose low-sounding monotone, eternally responding to some whisper of the infinite, mayhap lulls the dreamless sleepers beneath our feet.

Southward again, we come to historic old Plymouth, with its many Puritan shrines and associations, which did not prevent its becoming a shire-town of Transcendentalism. Here we see the house (framed in England, and erected here upside down) where Emerson, the fountain-head of that great "wave of spirituality," wooed and won Miss Jackson to be his wife; and not far away the lovely spot where, among his gardens, groves, and orchards, Marston Watson had his "Hillside" home,—to which resorted Emerson, Theodore Parker, Peabody, Thoreau, and Bronson Alcott, and which the latter celebrated in a sonnet. Here, too, we find the church where Kendall preached, and the farm of Morton, the earliest historian of the Western world.

In the Boston suburb of Jamaica Plain we find, near the station, the modest apartments where Miss Elizabeth Peabody—the " Saint Elizabeth" of her friends—passed her later years, and where, not many months ago, she died, having survived nearly all her associates in the earlier struggle for the enlargement of the bounds of spiritual freedom. She had been the intimate friend of Emerson, Channing, Theodore Parker, and the rest; and of the wider spirituality which they proclaimed she was esteemed a prophetess. Most of her literary work was done before she came to this home; and the latest literary effort of her life, her autobiography (which was undertaken here in age and weariness), was frustrated by her increasing infirmities.

In the same delightful suburb was the ideally beautiful home of the historian Francis Parkman. His wide and tasteful dwelling surmounted an elevation overlooking a pretty lakelet, and was environed by ample grounds filled with choicest shrubbery and flowers, where there were roods of the roses and lilies he loved

In and Out of Literary Boston.

and studied. In this place he lived thirty-four
years, and, although practically blind and rarely
free from torturing pain, he here produced many
volumes and accomplished the work which places
him among the foremost historians of the age.
In this home he died a year or so ago: his
grounds having been taken for a public park,
it is now proposed to erect here a bronze memorial of the great historian amid the floral beauty
he created and cherished.

In the remoter region of Canton, Thomas
Bailey Aldrich has a sometime summer home,
erected among enchanting landscapes, where he
has pondered and written much of his dainty
prose and daintier poesy. The curious name
of this rural retreat is preserved in the title
of his entertaining volume of travel-sketches,
"From Ponkapog to Pesth." The tree near
his door was the home of the pair of birds he
described in the delightful sketch "Our New
Neighbors at Ponkapog."

A morning's drive westward through the shade
and sheen of a delectable urban district conveys
us to the village of Auburndale, where we find
the tasteful cottage home of Louise Imogen
Guiney, with its French roofs, wide windows,
square tower, and embosoming foliage. Here, if
we come properly accredited, we may (or might

before she became the village postmistress) see the gifted poetess of " White Sail" and " Roadside Harp" and essayist of " English Gallery" and " Prose Idyls"—a *petite* and attractive young lady—at her desk, surrounded by her treasures of books and bric-à-brac and with the portraits of many friends looking down upon her from the walls of the square upper room where she writes. She has little to say concerning her own work,—fascinating as it is to her,—but discourses pleasantly on many topics and narrates *con amore* the history of the precious tomes and the literary relics she has gathered here, and describes the traits and lineage of her beloved canine pets, who have been execrated by some of her neighbors.

Nearer Jamaica Plain is the quiet corner of West Roxbury, where the exalted community of Brook Farmers attempted to realize in external and material fashion their high ideals and to inaugurate the precursor of an Arcadian era. In this season, "the sweet o' the year," we find the farm a delightful spot, fully warranting Hawthorne's eulogium in "Blithedale Romance." The songful stream which gives the place its name is margined by verdant and sun-kissed meads which slope away to the circling Charles; on either side, fields and picturesque pastures—

broken here and there by rocky ledges and copse-covered knolls—swell upward to feathery ac-clivities of pine and oak, with rugged escarp-ments of rock. From the elevation about the farm-house we overlook most of the domain of these social reformers,—the many acres of woodlands, the orchards and fields where Ripley, George William Curtis, Hawthorne, Dwight, Bedford, Pratt, Dana, and other transcendental enthusiasts held sublimated discourse while they performed the coarsest farm drudgery, applied uncelestial fertilizers, "belabored rugged fur-rows," or delved for the infinite in a peat-bog. Curtis has said "there never were such witty potato-patches, such sparkling corn-fields; the weeds were scratched out of the ground to the music of Tennyson and Browning." The farm-house stands above the highway, and is shaded by giant trees planted by Ripley and his asso-ciates. It is a commodious, antiquated structure of weather-worn wood, two stories in height, with a vast attic beneath the sloping roofs and an extension which has been recently enlarged. The original edifice is a ponderous fabric of almost square form, with an entrance in the mid-dle of the front, massive chimneys at either end, and contains four spacious lower rooms, besides an outer scullery. Here we see the sitting-room

of the reformers, where at first Channing sometimes preached and the now "Nestor of American journalism" sang bass in the choir; their
refectory, where Dana served as head-waiter;
and their brick-paved kitchen, where the erudite
Mrs. Ripley and the soulful Margaret Fuller
sometimes helped to prepare the bran bread and
baked beans for the exalted brotherhood. Adjoining is the old "wash-room," where some
who have since become famous in literature or
politics pounded the soiled linen in a hogshead
with a heavy wooden pestle; and just without
is the turf-carpeted yard where the dignified
and handsome Hawthorne, the brilliant Charles
A. Dana (who certainly was the most popular
member of the community), and the genial Curtis were sometimes seen hanging the moist gar-
ments upon the lines, a truly edifying spectacle
for gods and men. It was from Curtis's pockets
that the clothes-pins sometimes dropped during
the evening dances. Some of the trees yet to
be seen near the house were rooted from the
nursery established here by Dana.

This old house was the original "Hive" of
the community, who added the extensive wing
at the back, but increasing numbers soon forced
a portion of the company to swarm, and other
dormitories were erected. Of these we find ves-

tiges of the "Eyrie"—which was also used as a school-house—upon a commanding ledge at a little distance from the house, and nearer the grove where the rural festivals of the association were held. Of the "Nest," the little house where Miss Ripley lived, the "Cottage," where Margaret Fuller lodged during her sojourns at the farm, the large barn, where social *séances* were held while the starry company prepared vegetables for the market, and the other steading erected by the community, only the cellars and broken foundations remain. In the wood at some distance from the house is the "Eliot's Pulpit" of Coverdale's narrative, a mass of rock crowning a knoll and having a great fissure through its core ; in the forest beyond we may find "Coverdale's Walk," and the "Hermitage" where he heard by accident the colloquy of Westervelt and Zenobia.

After the day of Ripley's brilliant colony the broad acres of Brook Farm were tilled by the town poor, and—"to what base uses!"—the pretty cottage of Margaret Fuller became a loathsome small-pox pest-house; the rooms of the "Hive," after six years of familiarity with ideal refiners and reformers, became the abode of paupers, and at this day are aswarm with an odorous multitude of German orphans, wards of a Lutheran society that now owns the place.

While the pilgrim may find but few traces of the physical labors of the choice spirits who once inhabited this spot, the beneficent results of the mental and moral work here accomplished—especially among the young—are manifest and ineffaceable. These infertile fields yielded but scant returns for the manual toil of the optimistic philosophers, but their earnest strivings toward social and mental emancipation have borne abundant fruit.

IN BERKSHIRE WITH HAWTHORNE

THE GRAYLOCK AND HOOSAC REGION

THE Hawthorne pilgrimage has drawn us to many shrines: the sunny scenes of " The Marble Faun," the peaceful landscapes of " Our Old Home," the now busy city of " The Scarlet Letter," the elm-shaded Salem of " Dr. Grimshaw" and " The House of the Seven Gables," the Manse of the " Mosses," the Wayside of "Septimius Felton" and " The Dolliver Romance,"—these and many another resort of the subtile romancer, in the Old World and the New, have held our lingering feet.

Amid the splendors of a New England September we follow him into the " headlong Berkshire" of " Ethan Brand" and " Tanglewood Tales."

Hawthorne was more than most writers influenced by environment; the situations and circumstances under which his work was produced often determined its tone and color, while the persons, localities, and occurrences observed by his alert senses in the real world about him were skilfully wrought into his romance. His residence in Berkshire affected not only the books written there, but some subsequently produced, and the scenery of this loveliest corner of New England supplied the setting for many of his tales. Some of the best passages of his " American Note-Books" are records of his observations in this region,—sundry scenes, characters, and incidents being afterward literally transcribed therefrom into his fiction,—while a few of his shorter stories seem to have been suggested by legends once current in Berkshire. It passes, therefore, that for us the greatest charm of this realm of delights is that all its beauties—the grandeur of its mountains, the enchantment of its valleys, the glamour of its autumn woods, the sheen of its lakelets, the sapphire of its skies—serve to bring us into closer sympathy with Hawthorne, to whom these beauties were once a familiar vision.

He first came to Berkshire in the summer of 1838. For thirteen years he had bravely " waited for the world to know" him. His " Twice-Told Tales" had brought him little fame or money, but they had procured him the friend-

ship of the Peabodys, and it would appear that
he and the lovely Sophia already loved each
other. In a letter to her sister Elizabeth, written early in the summer, Sophia says, " Hawthorne came one morning for a take-leave call,
looking radiant. He said he was not going to
tell any one, not even his mother, where he
should be for the next months ; he thought he
should change his name, so that if he died no one
would be able to find his gravestone. We asked
him to keep a journal while he was gone. He
at first said he would not write anything, but
finally concluded it would suit very well for
hints for future stories." It was from his journal of these months of mysterious retirement
that, forty years later, the gentle Sophia—then
his widow—transcribed those pages of the
" Note-Books" which contain the account of his
sojourn in upper Berkshire and of his observations and meditations there. How far the journal
furnished " hints for future stories" the literary
world well knows.

A few days after this " take-leave call" we
find Hawthorne at Pittsfield, where his Berkshire saunterings (and ours) fitly began. We
follow him northward along a curving valley
hemmed by mountains that slope upward to the
azure ; on the right rise the rugged Hoosacs in

In Berkshire with Hawthorne

"Wave-like walls that block the sky
With tints of gold and mists of blue;"

on the left loom the darkly-wooded domes of
the Taconics above the bright upland pastures,
while before us grand old "Graylock" uprears
his head "shaggy with primeval forest,"—his
gigantic shape forming the culmination of the superb landscape.   Hawthorne's superlative pleasure of beholding this grandeur and beauty from
the driver's seat of a stage and being regaled at
the same time by the converse of the driver is
denied to us, but we enjoy quite as much as did
Hawthorne the little "love-pats" and passages
of a newly-wedded pair of our fellow-passengers.
The stage has disappeared, the driver and the
high-stepping steeds which served him "in
wheel and in whoa" have given place to the
engineer and the locomotive; the changes of
the half-century since Hawthorne journeyed
here have well-nigh overturned the world; only
the eternal beauty of these hills and the bewray-
ing demeanor of the newly-married remain evermore unchanged.

At North Adams, which the magician, "liking
indifferent well, made his head-quarters," we have
lodgings near the place of his on the Main Street
and in the domicile of one who, as a lad of fourteen

years, had known Hawthorne during his stay
here. Apparently he did not attempt to carry
out his plan of concealing his identity; he
certainly was known to some of the villagers as
the author of "Twice-Told Tales," and a de-
scendant of one of Hawthorne's "seven doctors
of the place" recalls his delight on being told
that the "Whig Tavern boarder" was the creator
of "The Gentle Boy;" and he remembers his
subsequent and consequent worshipful espionage
of the wonderful being. To this espionage we
are indebted for some edifying details of Hawthorne's sojourn in upper Berkshire. The world
has known few handsomer men than Hawthorne
was at this period of his life,—he had been
styled Oberon at college,—and our informant
recollects him as "the most brilliantly handsome
person he ever beheld," tall, dark, with an ex-
pressive mobile face and a lustrous eye which
held something "indescribably more than keen-
ness" in its quick glances. (Charles Reade said
Hawthorne's eye was "like a violet with a soul
in it.") As remembered here, his expression
was often abstracted, sometimes despondent.
He would sit for hours at a time on the broad
porch of the old "North Adams House," or in
a corner of the bar-room, silently smoking and
apparently oblivious to his surroundings, yet,

as we know, vigilant to note the oddities of character and opinion he encountered. It is certain that he did not drink immoderately at this time. There were a few persons—*not* the model men of the community—to whom he occasionally unbent and whom he admitted to a sort of comradeship, which, as his diary shows, often became confessionary upon their part. With these he held prolonged converse upon the tavern porch,—his part in the conversations being mainly suggestions calculated to elicit the whimsical conceits or experiences of his companions,—sitting the while in the posture of the venerable custom-house officials, described in the sketch introductory to the "Scarlet Letter," with "chair tipped on its hind legs" and his feet elevated against a pillar of the porch. Among those remembered to have been thus favored was Captain C——, called Captain Gavett in the "Note-Books," who dispensed metaphysics and maple sugar from the tavern steps, and a jolly blacksmith named Wetherel, described by Hawthorne as "big in the paunch and enormous in the rear," who came regularly to the bar for his stimulant. Another was the "lath-like, round-backed, rough-bearded, thin-visaged" stage-driver, Platt, whom Hawthorne honors as "a friend of mine" in the diary, and whose acquaintance he made during the ride from Pittsfield. In later years Platt's pride in having known Hawthorne eclipsed even his sense of distinction in being " the first and only man to drive an ox-team to the top of Graylock, sir." He had once been employed to haul the materials for an observatory up that mountain's steep inclines. Of the other " hangers-on" who were wont to infest the bar-room and porch fifty years ago and whom Hawthorne depicts in his journal and his fiction, few of the present generation of loungers in the place have ever heard. Orrin ——, the sportive widower whose peccadilloes are hinted at in the " Note-Books," is remembered by older residents of the town, and the " fellow who refused to pay six dollars for the coffin in which his wife was buried" may still be named as the personification of meanness. The maimed and dissolute Daniel Haines—nicknamed " Black Hawk"—was then a familiar figure in the village streets, and his unique history and appearance could not escape the notice of the great romancer nor be soon forgotten by the towns-people. As Hawthorne says, " he had slid down by degrees from law to the soap-vat." Once a reputable lawyer, his bibulous habits and an accident—his hand being " torn away by the devilish grip of a steam-engine"—had so reduced him that at the time Hawthorne saw him he maintained himself by boiling soap and practising phrenology. It is remembered that he used to "feel of bumps" for the price of a drink, and that, Hawthorne's head being submitted to his manipulation, he gravely assured the tavern company, "This man was created to shine as a bank president," and then privately advised the landlord to "make that chap pay in advance for his board." A resident tells us that this dirty and often drunken Haines used to make biweekly visits to his father's house, with a cart drawn by disreputable-looking dogs, to receive fat in exchange for soap. The novelist touches this odd character many times in his journal, and utilizes it in the romance of "Ethan Brand," where it is the "Lawyer Giles, the elderly ragamuffin," who, with the rest of the lazy regiment from the village tavern, came in response to the summons of the "boy Joe" to see poor Brand returned from his long search after the Unpardonable Sin. This "boy Joe," son of "Bertram the lime-burner," was also a bar-room character, noted here by Hawthorne, but obviously for a different use than that made of him in "Ethan Brand,"—a reference to him in the "Note-Books" being supplemented by this memoran-

dum: "take this boy as the germ of a tavern-
haunter, a country *roué,* to spend a wild and
brutal youth, ten years of his prime in prison
and his old age in the poor-house." This
sketch may have been written in the spirit of
prophecy, so exactly has the life of one bar-room
boy coincided with Hawthorne's outline; the
career of another lad whom he here saw and possibly had in mind was happier.

A modern hotel has replaced the "Whig
Tavern" of Hawthorne's time, and a new set of
habitués now frequent its bar-room; another
generation of fat men has succeeded the in-
dividuals whose breadth of back was a marvel
to the novelist, and in the increased population
of the place the "many obese" would no longer
provoke comment. The lapsing decades have
expanded the pretty and busy factory-village he
found into a prettier and busier factory-city
without materially changing its prevailing air.
The vigorous young city has not wholly out-
grown the "hollow vale" walled in by tower-
ing mountains; the aspect of its grand environment is therefore essentially unaltered, and it
chances that there is scarcely a spot, in or about
the town, which received the notice of Hawthorne which may not still be identified. It
is our crowning pleasure in the resplendent

In Berkshire with Hawthorne

autumn days to follow his thoughtful step and dreamy vision through town and country-side to the spots he frequented and described, thus sharing, in a way, his companionship and beholding through his eyes the beauties which he has depicted of mountain and vale, forest and stream. On the summit of a hill in the village cemetery, where white gravestones gleam amid the evergreens, the grave of a child at whose burial Hawthorne assisted is pointed out by one who was present with him. The well-known author-divine Washington Gladden, sometime preached in a near-by church. The ever-varying phases of the heights which look down upon the town—the wondrous play of light and shade upon the great sweeps of foliage which clothe the mountain-sides, the shadows chasing each other along the slopes and changing from side to side as the day declines, until the vale lies in twilight while the near summits are gilded with sunset gold, the exquisite cloud-effects as the fleecy masses drift above the ridges or cling to the higher peaks—were a never-failing source of pleasure to Hawthorne, as they are to the loiterer of this day. Every shifting of the point of view as we stroll in the town reveals a new aspect of its mountain ramparts and arouses fresh delight. Hawthorne thought the village itself most beautiful when clouds deeply shaded the mountains while sunshine flooded the valley and, by contrast, made streets and houses a bright, rich gold.

The investing mountains give to the place the "snug and insular" air which Hawthorne observed; from many points it seems completely severed from the rest of the world. On some dark days sombre banks of cloud settle along the ridges and apparently so strengthen and heighten the beleaguering walls that we recall Hawthorne's fancy that egress is impossible save by " climbing above the clouds." However, the railways tunnel the base of one mountain and curve around the flanks of others, while

"Old roads winding, as old roads will,"

find easy grades about and over the ramparts, so that the bustling "Tunnel-city" is by no means isolated from the outside world.

The rambles among and beyond these investing mountains, by which Hawthorne made himself and " Eustace Bright" of " Wonder-Book" and " Tanglewood Tales" familiar with " rough, rugged, broken, headlong" Berkshire, were usually solitary. The before-mentioned admirer of the " Gentle Boy" sometimes offered to guide the novelist to places of interest in the vicinage,

In Berkshire with Hawthorne

but he usually preferred to be alone with nature
and his own reveries. Once when the lad proposed to pilot him to the peak of Graylock,
Hawthorne replied he " did not care to soar so
high ; the Bellows-Pipe was sightly enough for
him." He visited the latter point many times ;
it is a long walk from the village, and once
he returned so late that the hotel was closed
for the night and our lad pommelled the door
for him until the landlord descended, in wrath
and confidentially scant attire, to admit the novelist.

One starless night we were guided to the kiln
of " Bertram the lime-burner" which Hawthorne visited with Mr. Leach,—one of several
kilns high up on the steep slope without the
town, where the marble of the mountain is
converted into snow-white lime. The graphic
imagery of the tale may all be realized here
upon the spot where it is laid. Amid the darkness, the iron door which encloses the glowing
limestone apparently opens into the mountain-
side, and seems a veritable entrance to the infernal regions whose lurid flames escape by
every crevice. The dark and silent figure, re-
vealed to us by the weird light, sitting and
musing before the kiln, is surely " Ethan Brand"
on his solitary vigil, intent on perilous thoughts

166

as he looks into the flame, or mutely listening to the fiend he has evoked from the fire to tell him of the Unpardonable Sin; or it is the same Brand returned to the foot of Graylock after eighteen years of weary searching abroad, to find the Sin in his own heart and to burn that heart into snowy whiteness and purity in the kiln he had watched so long. As we ponder the scene we would scarce be surprised to witness the approach of the village rabble led by Joe, the old Jew exhibiting his " peep-show" at the foot of the kiln, and the self-pursuing cur violently chasing his own shortened tail, or to hear the demoniac laughter of Brand which scattered the terror-stricken rabble in the surrounding darkness. Certain it is that, thirteen years before he wrote the tale, Hawthorne saw here, at a kiln on the foot-hill of Graylock, his " Bertram," and heard the legend of a demented creature who threw himself into the midst of the circle of fire. The name " Ethan Brand" was that of an old resident of Hawthorne's Salem.

The summit of Graylock, whose rugged beauty has been sung by Holmes, Thoreau, Bryant, and Fanny Kemble, had for Hawthorne a sort of fascination. From the streets of the village, from all the ways by which he sauntered through the country-side, his eyes were continually turning to that lofty height, observant of its ever-changing aspects. His diary of the time abounds with records of its phases, presented in varying conditions of cloud and sunshine and from different places of prospect, and of the fanciful impressions suggested to his subtile thought by each fresh and unfamiliar appearance. A walk repeatedly enjoyed by him is along a primitive road on the mountain-side to the southern end of The Notch,—"where it slopes upward to the skies,"—whence he could see most of the enchanting valley of Berkshire—with its lakes, embowered villages, and billowy expanses of upland and mead—extending between mountain-borders to the great Dome which looms across it sixty miles away. In the distance he could see the crags of Bryant's Monument Mountain—the " headless sphinx" of his own " Wonder-Book"—rising above the gleaming lake whose margin was to be his later home.

Our route to the peak of Graylock is that taken by Hawthorne and Thoreau through the savage cleft of The Notch. We follow up a dashing mountain-stream past a charming cascade beneath darkening hemlocks, then along a rough road by the houses whose inhabitants Hawthorne thought "ought to be temperance people"

Natural Bridge

from the quality of the water they gave him to drink. In the remoter parts of the glen a stranger-pedestrian is still a wonder, and will be regarded as curiously as was the romancer. From the extremity of The Notch, Graylock rises steeply, his sides clothed with forests, through which we climb to the summit and our reward. From the site of Thoreau's bivouac, where Fanny Kemble once declaimed Romeo and Juliet to a picnic party, we behold a scene of unrivalled vastness and beauty,—on every side peak soaring beyond peak until the shadowy outlines blend with the distant sky. The view ranges from Grand Monadnock and the misty Adirondacks to the Catskills, the Dome of Mount Washington, and the far-away hills of Connecticut, while at our feet smiles the bright valley, as beautiful as that in which Rasselas dwelt.

A mile from the town we find one of the most picturesque spectacles in New England, the Natural Bridge, to which Hawthorne came again and again during his sojourn in this region. Amid a grove of pines apparently rooted in the solid rock, a tributary of the Hoosac has, during measureless eons of time, worn in the white marble a chasm sixty feet deep and fifteen feet wide, spanned at one point by a beautifully arched mass which forms a bridge high above

169

the stream which frets along the rock-strewn
floor of the canyon. Within the ravine the
brook falls in a rainbow-crowned cascade, and
below this is a placid pool with margins of
polished marble, where Hawthorne once medi-
tated a bath, but, alarmed by the approach of
visitors, he hastily resumed his habiliments,
"not caring to be to them the most curious
part of the spectacle."

From the deep bed of the brook the gazer
looks heavenward between lofty walls of crys-
talline whiteness which seem to converge as they
rise, whose surmounting crags jutting from the
verge are crowned by sombre evergreens which
overhang the chasm and almost shut out the sky.
As we traverse the gorge whose wildness so
impressed Hawthorne and listen to the re-echo-
ing roar of the now diminished stream, we are
reminded of his conceit that the scene is "like
a heart that has been rent asunder by a torrent
of passion which has raged and left ineffaceable
traces, though now there is but a rill of feeling
at the bottom."

Our way back to the town is along a riotous
stream which took strong hold upon the liking
of the novelist, by which he often walked and
in whose cool depths he bathed. His brief
descriptions of its secluded and turbulent course,

through resounding hollows, amid dark woods, under pine-crowned cliffs,—" talking to itself of its own wild fantasies in the voice of solitude and the wilderness,"—although written at the time but for his own perusal, are among the gems of the language. Farther down, the boisterous stream is now subdued and harnessed by man and made to turn wheels of factories; its limpid waters are discolored by dye-stuffs; its beauty is lost with its freedom; it becomes useful and—ugly.

One day our excursion is into the romantic valley of the Deerfield by the old stage-road over the Hoosac range, the route which Hawthorne took with his friends Birch and Leach. The many turns by which the road accomplishes the ascent afford constantly varying vistas of the valley out of which we rise, and progressively widening prospects of the forest-clad mountains beyond. At the summit we are in the centre of the magnificent panorama of mountains—glowing now with autumnal crimson and gold—which extorted from Henry Clay the declaration that he had " never beheld anything so beautiful."

On the bare and wind-swept plain which lies along the summit are a few farm-dwellings. Among these at the time of Hawthorne's visit

In Berkshire with Hawthorne

—before the great tunnel had pierced the mountain and superseded the stage-route—was a homely wayside inn, afterward a farm-house, at whose bar passengers were wont to " wet their whistles." It may be assumed that the romancer and his companions failed not to conform to this time-honored custom, for it was in that rude bar-room—since a farm-kitchen—that Hawthorne met the itinerant Jew with a diorama of execrable scratchings which he carried upon his back and exhibited as " specimens of the fine arts ;" in that room also the novelist witnessed the whimsical performance of the usually sensible and sedate old dog, who periodically broke out in an infuriated pursuit of his own tail, " as if one half of his body were at deadly enmity with the other." These incidents were carefully noted at the time for possible future use, and in such choice diction that when, many years afterward, he wove them into the fabric of a tale of " The Snow Image" volume, he transcribed them from his diary to his manuscript essentially unchanged. This instance illustrates the method of this consummate literary artist and his alertness to perceive and utilize the details of real life. His journals abundantly show that he was by no means the aphelxian dreamer he has been adjudged.

Deerfield Arch—Williamstown

As we descend into the deep valley we find a wild gulf where a brooklet from the top of Hoosac falls a hundred feet into a rock-bordered pool, whence it hastens to lose itself in the river; and a mile or two farther along the Deerfield we come to the Natural Arch which Hawthorne visited. It is in one of the wildest parts of the picturesque valley, where mountain-walls rise a thousand feet on either side. Through a mass of rock projecting from the margin the stream has wrought for itself a symmetrically arched passage as large as and very like the doorway of an Old-World cathedral. The summit of the arch and the water-worn pillars upon either side display "pot-holes" and other evidences of erosion, and in the bed of the current lie fragments of similarly attrite rocks which seem to indicate that at some period a series of arches spanned the entire space from mountain to mountain. Hawthorne's pleasing fancy makes this arch the entrance to an enchanted palace which has all vanished except the door-way that "now opens only into nothingness and empty space."

On other days our saunterings follow Hawthorne's to beautiful Williamstown and through the picturesque scenery which environs it. Within the park-like village the alma mater of

In Berkshire with Hawthorne

Bryant, Garfield, and Hawthorne's "Eustace Bright" stands embowered in noble elms and overlooked by mighty Graylock. Viewed from here, Emerson thought Graylock "a serious mountain." Thoreau considered its proximity worth at least "one endowed professorship; it were as well to be educated in the shadow of a mount as in more classic shades. Some will remember not only that they went to the college but that they went to the mountain." Hawthorne visited both. At the college commencement we find him more attentive to the eccentric characters in the assemblage without the church than to the literary exercises within, as evidenced by his piquant description of the enterprising pedler with the "heterogeny" of wares, the gingerbread man, the negroes, and other oddities of the out-door company.

About us here lie the scenes which stirred in William Cullen Bryant that intense love of nature which inspired his best stanzas. A winsome walk brings us to a sequestered glen where a brooklet winds amid moss-covered rocks and dainty ferns, and mirrors in its clear pools the overhanging boughs and the patches of azure; this was a favorite haunt of the youthful Bryant, and here he pondered or composed his earlier poems, including some portion of the matchless

" Thanatopsis." Here Emerson, lingering un
der the spell of the spot, was moved to recite
Wordsworth's " Excursion" to a companion,
who must evermore feel an enviable thrill when
he recalls the exquisite lines falling from the
lips of the " great evangel and seer" amid the
loveliness of such a scene.

LENOX AND MIDDLE BERK-SHIRE

---

*Beloved of the Littérateurs — La Maison Rouge — Where
The House of the Seven Gables was written—Wonder-
Book and Tanglewood Scenes — The Bowl — Beecher's
Laurel Lake — Kemble — Bryant's Monument Mountain —
Stockbridge — Catherine Sedgwick — Melville's Piazza
and Chimney — Holmes — Longfellow — Pittsfield.*

WE have only to accompany Eustace Bright
of "Wonder-Book" from Williams College to his home, where Catherine Sedgwick's
"Stockbridge Bowl" nestles among the summer-
enchanted hills of central Berkshire, to find the
abode of Hawthorne during the most fertile
period of his life. This region of inspiring
landscapes has long been a favorite residence of
littérateurs. Here Jonathan Edwards compiled
his predestined treatises; here Catherine Sedgwick wrote the romances which charmed her
generation; here Elihu Burritt "the Learned
Blacksmith," wrought out the "Sparks" that
made him famous; here Bryant composed his
best stanzas and made Monument Mountain and
Green River classic spots; here Henry Ward
Beecher indited many "Star Papers;" here Her-

man Melville produced his sea-tales and brilliant essays; here Headley and Holmes, Lowell and Longfellow, Curtis and James, Audubon and Whipple, Mrs. Sigourney and Martineau, Fanny Kemble and Frederika Bremer, the gifted sisters Goodale, and many other shining spirits, have had home or haunt and have invested the scenery with the splendors of their genius. Half a score of this galaxy were in Berkshire at the time of Hawthorne's residence there.

After his sojourn in northern Berkshire he returned to Salem, where he married the lovely Sophia Peabody, endured some years of custom-house drudgery, and wrote the " Scarlet Letter," which made him famous: he then sought again the seclusion of the mountains.

Poverty, which he had long and bravely endured, has been assigned as the cause of his removal to the humble Berkshire abode in 1850; one writer refers to the slenderness of his larder here, another says the rent for his poor dwelling was paid by his friends, another that the rent was remitted by the owner, who was his friend. But the success of the " Scarlet Letter" had relieved the necessitous condition of its author; and his landlord here—Tappan of " Tanglewood"— testifies and Hawthorne's letters show that he was able to pay his rent. His motive in returning to Berkshire is stated in a letter to Bridge : " I have taken a house in Lenox—I long to get into the country, for my health is not what it has been. An hour or two of labor in a garden and a daily ramble in country air would keep me all right." Doubtless, too, he hoped to find the quiet and seclusion of the place favorable for his work.

The habitation to which he brought his family he describes as " the very ugliest little bit of an old red farm-house you ever saw," " the most inconvenient and wretched hovel I ever put my head in." His wife's letters characterize it, " the reddest and smallest of houses," with such a low stud that she " fears to be crushed."

In later years we have found it scarcely changed since Hawthorne's occupancy ; it was indeed of the humblest and plainest,—a low-eaved, one-and-a-half-storied structure, with a lower wing at the side, dingy red in color, with window-shutters of green. The interior was cosy and more commodious than the exterior would indicate, and one could readily conceive that the artistic taste and deft fingers of Mrs. Hawthorne might create here the idyllic home her letters portray. We have been indebted to the courtesy of Hawthorne's friend Tappan for glimpses of the rooms which Mrs. Hawthorne had already made familiar to us: the tiny reception-room, where she "sewed at her stand and read to the children about Christ;" the drawing-room, where she disposed "the embroidered furniture," and where, in the farther corner, stood "Apollo with his head tied on;" the dining-room, where the "Pembroke table stood between the windows;" the small boudoir, with its enchanting outlook; the "golden chamber" where the baby Rose was born; the room of the "little lady Una;" and the low, dingy apartment which was the study of the master-genius. Of this room she says, "it can boast of nothing but his presence in the morning and the picture out of the window in the evening." His secretary was so placed that as he sat at his work he could look out upon a landscape of forest and meadow, lake and mountain, as beautiful as a poet's dream. It was the exquisite loveliness of this scene—which Hawthorne thought surpassed all others in Berkshire —that for a time reconciled him to the deficiencies of his situation here.

Monument Mountain, looming almost across the valley, is the most prominent feature of this view, and it was from his study window that he noted most of its varying aspects which are depicted in the " Wonder-Book" and in his letters and journals. Its contour is to him that of a " huge, headless sphinx," and when—as on the days we beheld it from his window—it blazes from base to summit with the resplendent hues of autumn, his fancy suggested that " the sphinx is wrapped in a rich Persian shawl;" with the sunshine upon it, " it has the aspect of burnished copper;" now it has " a fleece of sun-brightened mist," again it seems " founded on a cloud;" on other days it is " enveloped as if in the smoke of a great battle." Upon the pane through which he had looked upon these changeful phases his hand inscribed, " Nathaniel Hawthorne, February 9, 1851."

He could scarcely have found a lovelier location for his home. The valley, which sometimes seemed to him "a vast basin filled with sunshine as with wine," is enclosed by groups of mountains piled and terraced to the horizon. As we behold them in the splendor of the October days, great patches of sunshine and sable cloud-shadows flit along the glowing slopes in the sport of the wind. On the one side, the ground sweeps upward from the cottage site to the " Bald Summit" of the " Wonder-Book;" on the other, a meadow—as long as the finger of the giant of " Three Golden Apples"—slopes

to the lake a furlong distant. That beautiful
water, sung by Sigourney, Sedgwick, and Fanny
Kemble, stretches its bays three miles among
the hills to the southward and mirrors its own
wooded margins and the farther mountains.
Beyond the lake, rising in mid-air like a great
gray wall, are the sheer precipices of Monument Mountain, and in the hazy distance the
loftier Taconics uprear their grand Dome in the
illimitable blue.

Of "La Maison Rouge" of Hawthorne's
letters, the pilgrim of to-day finds only the
blackened and broken foundation walls: a de-
vouring fire, from which Tappan saved little of
his furniture, has laid it low. These walls
(which remain only because relic-hunters cannot
easily carry them away) measurably indicate the
form and dimensions of the cottage and its general arrangement. Its site is close upon the
highway, from which it is partially screened by
evergreen trees. The gate of the enclosure is
of course an unworthy successor to that upon
which Fields found Hawthorne swinging his
children, but these near-by elms have shaded
the great romancer, the tallest of the evergreens
is the tree his wife thought "full of a thousand
memories," and all about the spot cluster re-
minders of the simple, healthful life Hawthorne

In Berkshire with Hawthorne

led here. Here are the garden ground he tilled
and where he buried the pet rabbit "Bunny;"
the "patch," ploughed for him by Tappan,
where he raised beans for himself and corn for
his hens (he had learned something of agriculture at Brook Farm, albeit it was said there he
could do nothing but feed the hogs); the now
great fruit-trees whose leaden labels little Julian
destroyed, as Tappan remembers; the place of
the "scientific hennery," fitted up by the "Man
of Genius and the Naval Officer,"—Hawthorne
and Horatio Bridge; the long declivity where
the novelist as well as his Eustace Bright used
to coast "in the nectared air of winter" with
the children of the "Wonder-Book;" the leafy
woods—his refuge from visitors—where he
walked with his children and where Bright
nutted with the little Pringles; the lake-shore
where Hawthorne loitered or lay extended in
the shade during summer hours, "smoking cigars,
reading foolish novels, and thinking of nothing
at all," while the children played about him or
covered his chin and breast with long grasses to
make him "look like the mighty Pan."

Near by are other friends he has made known
to us. Yonder copse shades a narrow glen
whose braes border a brooklet winding and
chattering on its way to the lake; this glen was

a summer haunt of Hawthorne, where he doubt-less pondered much of his work. Here he brought his children " to play with the brook" and helped them to build water-falls, or reclined in the shade and told them stories as described in the " Wonder-Book,"—for this is the " dell of Shadow-Brook," where the children picnicked with Bright and where he told them the story of " The Golden Touch" on such an afternoon as this, on which we behold the dell thickly strewn with golden leaves, as if King Midas had newly emptied his coffers there.

Yonder mansion of Hawthorne's landlord, just beyond the highway, is " Tanglewood," —place of the Pringles' home and still the abode of Tappan's daughters,—where Bright spent his vacations and where Hawthorne makes him tell many of the " Tales." The view de-scribed on the porch, where the " Gorgon's Head" was narrated, is the one Hawthorne saw from his study window. Glimpses of various rooms of the mansion which Tappan then in-habited and called " Highwood" are prefixed to the stories told in them. Beyond " Tangle-wood" steeply rises an eminence whose bare acclivity Hawthorne often climbed with his family,—the " Bald Summit" where the Pringles listened to the tale of " The Chimera." We

In Berkshire with Hawthorne

ascend by the novelist's accustomed way "through Luther Butler's orchard," and are repaid by a view extending from the mountains of Vermont to the Catskills and deserving the high praise Hawthorne bestowed. A golden cloud floating close to Graylock's shaggy head reminds us of Hawthorne's conceit that a mortal might step from the mountain to the cloud and thus ascend heavenly heights. The farther ranges enclose a valley of wave-like hills,—which look as if a tumultuous ocean had been transfixed and solidified,—dotted with farmsteads and picturesque villages whose white spires rise from embowering trees. At our feet the "Bowl" ripples and scintillates, farther away the "Echo Lake" of Christine Nilsson and many smaller lakelets "open their blue eyes to the sun," while the placid stream, fringed by overhanging willows, circles here and there through the valley like a shining ribbon. Here we may realize the immensity of Hawthorne's giant in the "Three Golden Apples," who was so tall he "might have seated himself on Taconic and had Monument Mountain for a footstool."

Not far away, near another shore of the shimmering "Bowl," that versatile genius "Carl Benson"—Charles Astor Bristed—dwelt for some time in a quaint old farm-house which has since been destroyed by fire, and here accomplished some of his literary work. Laurel Lake (the Scott's Pond of Hawthorne's "Note-Books"), where Beecher "bought a hundred acres to lie down upon,"—and called them Blossom Farm in the "Star Papers" written there,—was another resort of Hawthorne. We find it a pretty water, although its margins are mostly denuded of large trees. A bright matron of the vicinage, who, when a child, thought the author of the "Wonder-Book" the "greatest man in the world save only Franklin Pierce," lived then by Hawthorne's road to Laurel Lake. Her admiration for him (heightened by his intimacy with Pierce) led her to daily watch the road by which he would come from Tanglewood, and when she saw him approaching—which would be twice a week in good weather—she would go into the yard and reverently gaze at him until his swift gait had carried him out of sight. To her he was a tall, dark man with a handsome clean-shaven face and lustrous eyes which saw nothing but the ground directly before him, habitually dressed in black, with a wide-brimmed soft hat. Usually his walk was solitary, but sometimes Herman Melville, who was well known in the neighborhood, was his companion, and one autumn he was twice or

thrice accompanied by "a light spare man,"—
the poet Ellery Channing.   Once Hawthorne
strode past toward the lake when Fanny Kemble,
who lived near by, rode her black steed by his
side and "seemed to be doing all the talking"
—she was capable of that—and "was talking
politics."   Having secured a Democratic auditor,
she doubtless "improved the occasion" with
her habitual vivaciousness.   A neighbor of Hawthorne's tells us this incident of the following
year, when the novelist's friend Pierce had been
named for the Presidency.   One dark night this
neighbor went on foot to a campaign lecture at
Lenox Furnace.   At its close, he essayed to
shorten the homeward walk by a "short cut"
across the fields, and, of course, lost his way.
Descrying a light, he directed his steps toward
it, but found himself involved in a labyrinth of
obstacles, and had to make so many détours that
when he finally reached the house whence the
light proceeded, and when in response to his
hail the door was opened by Kemble herself,
he was so distraught and amazed at being lost
among his own farms that he could hardly ex-
plain his plight; but she quickly interrupted
his incoherent account: "Yes, I see, poor be-
nighted man! you've been to a Democratic
meeting; no wonder you are bewildered!   Now

Fanny Kemble—Monument Mountain

I'll lend you a good Whig lantern that will light you safe home." We find Mrs. Kemble-Butler's "Perch"—as she named her home here—a little enlarged, but not otherwise changed since the time of her occupancy. She was a general favorite, and her dark steed, which had cost her the proceeds of a volume of her poems, used to stop before every house in the vicinage. She often came, habited in a sort of bloomer costume which shocked some of her friends, to fish in the "Bowl" at the time Hawthorne dwelt by its shore.

The death of Louis Kossuth, some time ago, reminded her former neighbors here that she led the dance with him at a ball in Lenox, when the exiled patriot was a guest of the Sedgwicks.

Our approach to Monument Mountain is along one of those sequestered by-ways which Hawthorne loved, with "an unseen torrent roaring at an unseen depth" near by. A rift in the morning mists which enshroud the valley displays the mountain summit bathed in sunshine. We ascend by Bryant's "path which conducts up the narrow battlement to the north," the same along which Hawthorne and his friends— Holmes, James T. Fields, Sedgwick, and the rest—were piloted by the historian Headley on a summer's day more than forty years ago. Standing upon the beetling verge, which is scarred and splintered by thunderbolts and overhangs a precipice of five hundred feet or more, we look abroad upon a landscape of wondrous expanse and beauty. Here we may realize all the prospect Bryant portrayed as he stood upon this spot:

> " A beautiful river
> Wanders amid the fresh and fertile meads ;
>   On either side
> The fields swell upward to the hills ; beyond,
> Above the hills, in the blue distance, rise
> The mighty columns with which earth props heaven."

In the middle distance, across the Bowl, which gleams a veritable "mountain mirror," we see the site of the home whence Hawthorne so often looked upon these cliffs. Yonder detached pinnacle, rising from the base of the precipice beneath us, is the "Pulpit Rock" which Catherine Sedgwick christened when Hawthorne's party picnicked here ; from the crag projecting from the verge Fanny Kemble declaimed Bryant's poem, and Herman Melville, bestriding the same rock for a bowsprit, "pulled and hauled imaginary ropes" for the amusement of the company. Among these splintered masses the company lunched that day and drank quantities of Heidsieck to the health of the "dear old poet of Monument Mountain." On the east, almost within sight from this eminence, is the spot where he was born, near the birthplaces of Warner and the gifted Mrs. Howe.

Another day we follow the same brilliant party of Hawthorne's friends through the Stockbridge Ice Glen,—a narrow gorge which cleaves a rugged mountain from base to summit, its riven sides being apparently held asunder by immense rocky masses hurled upon each other in wild confusion. Beneath are weird grottos and great recesses which the sun never penetrates, and within these we make our way—clambering and sliding over huge boulders—through the heart of the mountain. One of Hawthorne's company here testifies that in all the extemporaneous jollity of the scramble through the glen the usually silent novelist was foremost, and, being sometimes in the dark, dared use his tongue,—"calling out lustily and pretending that certain destruction threatened us all. I never saw him in better spirits than throughout this day."

From the glen we trace Hawthorne to the staid old house of Burr's boyhood, where lived and wrote Jonathan Edwards, and the statelier dwelling whence Catherine Sedgwick gave her tales to the world. Near by we find the grave where she lies amid the scenes of her own "Hope Leslie," and not far from the sojourn of her gifted niece whose translation of Sand's "Fadette" has been so well received. Overlooking the village is the summer residence of Field of the "Evangelist,"—author of the delightful books of travel.

Farther away is a little farm-house, with a "huge, corpulent, old Harry VIII. of a chimney," to which Hawthorne was a frequent visitor,—the "Arrow-Head" of Herman Melville. "Godfrey Graylock" says the friendship between Hawthorne and Melville originated in their taking refuge together, during an electric shower, in a narrow cleft of Monument Mountain. They had been coy of each other on account of Melville's review of the "Scarlet Letter" in Duyckinck's *Literary World*, but during some hours of enforced intercourse and propinquity in very contracted quarters they discovered in each other a correlation of thought and feeling which made them fast friends for life. Thereafter Melville was often at the little red house, where the children knew him as "Mr. Omoo," and less often Hawthorne came to chat with the racy romancer and philosopher by the great chimney. Once he was accompanied by little Una—"Onion" he sometimes called her—and remained a whole week. This visit—certainly unique in the life of the shy Hawthorne—was the topic when, not so long agone, we last looked upon the living face of Melville in his city home. March weather prevented walks abroad, so the pair spent most of the week in smoking and talking metaphysics in the barn,—Hawthorne usually lounging upon a carpenter's bench. When he was leaving, he jocosely declared he would write a report of their psychological discussions for publication in a volume to be called " A Week on a Work-Bench in a Barn," the title being a travesty upon that of Thoreau's then recent book, " A Week on Concord River," etc.

Sitting upon the north piazza, of " Piazza Tales," at Arrow-Head, where Hawthorne and his friend lingered in summer days, we look away to Graylock and enjoy " the calm prospect of things from a fair piazza" which Melville so whimsically describes. At Arrow-Head, too, we find the astonishing chimney which suggested the essay, still occupying the centre of the house and " leaving only the odd holes and corners" to Melville's nieces, who now inhabit the place in summer; the study where Hawthorne and Melville discussed the plot of the " White Whale" and other tales; the great fireplace, with its inscriptions from "I and my Chimney;" the window-view of Melville's "October Mountain,"—beloved of Longfellow,—whose autumn glories inspired that superb word-picture and metaphysical sketch.

On a near knoll, commanding a view of the circle of mountains and the winding river, stands the sometime summer residence of Holmes among his ancestral acres, where Hawthorne and Fields came to visit him. His "den," in which he did much literary work, overlooks the beautiful meadows, and is now expanded into a large library, while the trees he planted are grown to be the crowning beauty of the place, which the owner calls Holmesdale. It was the hereditary home of the Wendells.

Beyond, at the edge of the town of Pittsfield, is the mansion where Longfellow found his wife and his famous "Old Clock on the Stairs." At the Athenæum in the town some thousands of Holmes's books will soon be placed, and here is preserved the secretary from Hawthorne's study in the little red house,—a time-worn mahogany combination of desk, drawers, and shelves, at which he wrote "The House of the Seven Gables," "The Wonder-Book," "The Snow Image," and part of "The Blithedale Romance." Pittsfield was long the home of

Hawthorne's Habit of Meditation

"Godfrey Graylock;" here the gifted Rose Terry Cooke passed her closing years of life with her husband, and not far away Josh Billings, "the Yankee Solomon," was born and reared as Henry Savage Shaw. One day we trace from Pittsfield the footsteps of Hawthorne and Melville across the Taconics to the whilom home of "Mother Ann" and to the higher Hancock peaks.

Hawthorne's daily walk to the post-office was past the later residence of Charlotte Cushman, and by the church where the older Channing delivered his last discourse and where twenty years ago Parkhurst was preacher. In the church-tower Fanny Kemble's clock still tells the hours above the lovely spot where she desired to be buried.

These various excursions compass the range of Hawthorne's rambles in this region : he was never ten miles away from the little red house during his residence here. Obviously he preferred short and solitary strolls which allowed undisturbed meditation upon the work in hand. The quantity and finish of the writing done here indicate that much thought was expended upon it outside his study. We may be sure that upon " The House of the Seven Gables" were bestowed, besides the five months of daily sessions at his desk, other months of study and thought as he strolled the country roads and loitered by the lake-side or in the dell of " Blossom-Brook." He avowed himself a shameless idler in warm weather, declaring he was " good for nothing in a literary way until after the autumnal frosts" brightened his imagination as they did the foliage about him here; yet the meditations of one summer in Berkshire produced his masterpiece, and the next summer accomplished " The Wonder-Book," quickly followed by " The Snow Image" and " Blithedale." During this summer also he had a voluminous correspondence with the many " Pyncheon jackasses" who thought themselves aggrieved by his use of their name in " The House of the Seven Gables."

Of the simple home-life at the little red house, Hawthorne's diaries and letters, as well as some of the books written here, afford pleasing glimpses. The " Violet" and " Peony" of the "Snow Image" story are the novelist's own little Una and Julian, and the tale was suggested by some occurrence in their play; the incidents related of Eustace Bright and the young Pringles, which are prefixed to the " Wonder-Book" stories, are merely experiences of Hawthorne and his children, and during the composition of these tales he delighted these children—as

Life in the Little Red House

one of them remembers—by reading to them each evening the work of the day. A grim-visaged negress named Peters, who was the servant here in the little red house, is said to have suggested the character of Aunt Keziah in "Septimius Felton."

Hawthorne's chickens receive notice as members of the family in his diary,—thus: "Seven chickens hatched, J. T. Headley called—eight chickens;" "ascended a mountain with my wife, eight more chickens hatched." In a letter to Horatio Bridge, "Our children grow apace and so do our chickens;" "we are so intimate with every individual chicken that it seems like cannibalism to think of eating one of them." Hawthorne's daily walk with pail in hand to Luther Butler's, the next farm-house, he speaks of as his "milky way." Butler lives now two miles distant. The novelist thus announces to his friend Bridge the birth of the present gifted poetess, Mrs. Lathrop, the daughter of his age: "Mrs. Hawthorne has published a little work which still lies in sheets, but makes some noise in the world; it is a healthy miss with no present pretensions to beauty." Five cats were cherished by the novelist and his children; a snowy morning after Hawthorne's removal, three of the cats came to a neighboring house, where their descendants are still petted and cherished.

A few visitors came to the little red house—Kemble, James, Lowell, Holmes, E. P. Whipple, and the others already mentioned—in whose presence the "statue of night and silence" was wont to relax, but for the most part his life was that of a recluse. Here, as elsewhere, his thoughts dwelt apart in "a twilight region" where the company of his kind was usually a perturbing intrusion. For companionship, his family, the lake, the woods, his own thoughts, sufficed; he seldom sought any other, and therefore was unpopular in the neighborhood. It is hardly to be supposed that the creator of Zenobia, Hester Prynne, and the Pyncheons would greatly enjoy the society of his rural neighbors, but they were not therefore the less displeased by his habitually going out of his way—sometimes across the fields—to avoid meeting them. Some of them had a notion that he was the author of "a poem, or an arithmetic, or some other kind of a book,"—as he makes "Primrose Pringle" to say of him in the tale,—but to most he was incomprehensible, perhaps a little uncanny, and the great genius of romance is yet mentioned here as "a queer sort o' man that lived in Tappan's red house."

Reasons for leaving Berkshire

His son records that after Hawthorne had freed himself from Salem "he soon wearied of any particular locality;" after a time he tired even of beautiful Berkshire. Its obtrusive scenery "with the same strong impressions repeated day after day" became irksome; then he grew tired of the mountains and "would joyfully see them laid flat." He writes to Fields, "I am sick of Berkshire, and hate to think of spending another winter here." Doubtless the region which we behold in the glamour of the early autumn seemed very different to Hawthorne in the season when he had daily "to trudge two miles to the post-office through snow or slush knee-deep." Ellery Channing—who had knowledge of the winter here—in his letters to Hawthorne calls Berkshire "that satanic institution of Spitzbergen," "that ice-plant of the Sedgwicks."

A more cogent reason for Hawthorne's discontent here is found in his failing health. He writes to Pike, "I am not vigorous as I used to be on the coast;" to Fields, "For the first time since boyhood I feel languid and dispirited. Oh, that Providence would build me the merest shanty and mark me out a rood or two of garden near the coast."

For these and other reasons Hawthorne finally left Berkshire at the end of 1851, going first to

In Berkshire with Hawthorne

West Newton and a few months later to "the Wayside," while his friend Tappan occupied the thenceforth famous little red house.

The world of readers owes much to Hawthorne's residence among the mountains. Besides the material here gathered and the exquisite settings for his tales these landscapes afforded, we are indebted to his environment in Berkshire for the quality of the work here accomplished and for its quantity as well; for he responded so readily to the inspiriting influence of his surroundings that he produced more during his stay here than at any similar period of his life. The soulful beauty and the seclusion of the haunts to which we here trace him, suiting well his solitary mood, may measurably account to us for his habit of thought and for the manner of expression by which nature was here portrayed and life expounded by the great master of American romance.

A DAY WITH THE GOOD GRAY POET

A DAY WITH THE GOOD
GRAY POET

Walk and Talk with Socrates in Camden — The Bard's Appearance and Surroundings — Recollections of his Life and Work — Hospital Service — Praise for his Critics — His Literary Habit, Purpose, Equipment, and Style — His Religious Bent — Readings.

"HOW can you find him? Nothing is easier," quoth the Philadelphia friend who some time before Whitman's death brought us an invitation from the bard; "you have only to cross the ferry and apply to the first man or woman you meet, for there is no one in Camden who does not know Walt Whitman or who would not go out of his way to bring you to him." The event justifies the prediction, for when we make inquiry of a tradesman standing before a shop, he speedily throws aside his apron, closes his door against evidently needed customers, and—despite our protest—sets out to conduct us to the home of the poet. This is done with such obvious ardor that we hint to our guide that he must be one of the "Whitmaniacs," whereupon he rejoins, "I never read a word Whitman wrote. I don't know why they call him Socrates, but I do know he never passes me

A Day with the Good Gray Poet

without a friendly nod and a word of greeting that warms me all through." We subsequently find that it is this sort of "Whitmania," rather than that Swinburne deplores, which pervades the vicinage of the poet's home.

Our conductor leaves us at the door of three hundred and twenty-eight Mickle Street, a neat thoroughfare bordered by unpretentious frame dwellings, hardly a furlong from the Delaware. The dingy little two-storied domicile is so disappointingly different from what we were expecting to see that the confirmatory testimony of the name "W. Whitman" upon the door-plate is needed to convince us that this is the oft-mentioned "neat and comfortable" dwelling of one of the world's celebrities.

We are kept waiting upon the door-step long enough to observe that the unpainted boards of the house are weather-worn and that the shabby window-shutters and the cellar-door, which opens aslant upon the sidewalk, are in sad need of repair, and then we are admitted by the "good, faithful, young Jersey woman who," as he lovingly testifies, "cooks for and vigilantly sees to" the venerable bard. A moment later we are in his presence, in the spacious second-story room which is his sleeping apartment and work-room.

Whitman's Personal Appearance

"You are good to come early while I am fresh and rested," exclaims Walt Whitman, rising to his six feet of burly manhood and advancing a heavy step or two to greet us; "we are going to have a talk, and we have something to talk about, you know," referring to a literary venture of ours which had procured us the invitation to visit him. When he has regained the depths of his famous and phenomenal chair, the "Jersey woman" hands him a score of letters, which he offers to lay aside, but we insist that he shall read them at once, and while he is thus occupied we have opportunity to observe more closely the bard and his surroundings.

We see a man made in massive mould, stalwart and symmetrical,—not bowed by the weight of time nor deformed by the long years of hemiplegia; a majestic head, large, leonine, Homeric, crowned with a wealth of flowing silvery hair; a face like "the statued Greek" (Bucke says it is the noblest he ever saw); all the features are full and handsome; the forehead, high and thoughtful, is marked by "deep furrows which life has ploughed;" the heavy brows are highly arched above eyes of gray-blue which in repose seem suave rather than brilliant; the upper lid droops over the eye nearly to the pupil,—a condition which obtains in partial ptosis,—and we

afterward observe that when he speaks of mat-
ters which deeply move him his eyelids have a
tendency to decline still farther, imparting to
his eyes an appearance of lethargy altogether at
variance with the thrilling earnestness and tre-
mor of his voice. A strong nose, cheeks round
and delicate, a complexion of florid and transparent pink,—its hue being heightened by the
snowy whiteness of the fleecy beard which
frames the face and falls upon the breast. The
face is sweet and wholesome rather than refined,
vital and virile rather than intellectual. Joa-
quin Miller has said that, even when destitute
and dying, Whitman "looked like a Titan
god."

We think the habitual expression of his face
to be that of the sage benignity that comes with
age when life has been well lived and life's work
well done. The expression bespeaks a soul at
ease with itself, unbroken by age, poverty, and
disease, unsoured by calumny and insult. Certainly his buffetings and his brave endurance of
wrong have left no record of malice or even of
impatience upon his kindly face. His manly
form is clad in a loosely fitting suit of gray; his
rolling and ample shirt-collar, worn without a
tie, is open at the throat and exposes the upper
part of his breast; all his attire, "from snowy

linen to burnished boot," is scrupulously clean and neat.

His room is of generous proportions, occupying nearly the entire width of the house, and lighted by three windows in front. The floor is partly uncarpeted, and the furniture is of the simplest; his bed, covered by a white counterpane, occupies a corner; there are two large tables; an immense iron-bound trunk stands by one wall and an old-fashioned stove by another; a number of boxes and uncushioned seats are scattered through the apartment; on the walls are wardrobe-hooks, shelves, and many pictures, —a few fine engravings, a print of the Seminole Osceola, portraits of the poet's parents (his father's face is a good one) and sisters, and of "another—not a sister."

There are many books here and there, some of them well worn; one corner holds several Greek and Latin classics and copies of Burns, Tennyson, Scott, Ossian, Emerson, etc. On the large table near his chair are his writing materials, with the Bible, Shakespeare, Dante, and the Iliad within reach. Bundles of papers lie in odd places about the room; piles of books, magazines, and manuscripts are heaped high upon the tables, litter the chairs, and overflow and encumber the floor. This room holds

A Day with the Good Gray Poet

what Whitman has called the "storage collection" of his life.

"And now you are to tell me about yourself
and your work," says the poet, pushing aside
his letters. But, although he is the best of lis-
teners, we are intent to make him talk, and a
fortunate remark concerning one of his letters
which had seemed to interest him more than
the others—it came from a friend of his far-away
boyhood—enables us to profit by the reminiscential mood the letter has inspired.

In his low-toned voice he pictures his early
home, his parents, and his first ventures into the
world; with evident relish he narrates his ludicrous experience when he—a stripling school-
master—"went boarding 'round." Than this,
there was but one happier period of his life,
and that was when he drove among the farms
and villages distributing his *Long Islander:*
"that was bliss."

Later he was a politician and "stumped the
island" for the Democratic candidates, but the
enactment of the fugitive slave law disgusted
him, and he declared his political emancipation
in the poem "Blood-Money." At odd times
he has done "a deal of newspaper drudgery"
and other work, but his "forte always was loaf-
ing and writing poetry,—at least until the war."

He began early to clothe his thought in verse, and was but a lad when a poem of his was accepted for publication in the New York *Mirror*, and he depicts for us the surprised delight with which he beheld his stanzas in that fashionable journal.

A pleasure of those early years was the companionship of Bryant, and he details to us the "glorious walks and talks" they had together along the North Shore in sweet summer days. This, he says with a sigh, was the dearest of the friendships lost to him by the publication of "Leaves of Grass;" "but there were compensations, Emerson and Tennyson." Of later events he speaks less freely. Of the years of devoted service to the wounded and dying in army hospitals, when day and night he literally gave himself for others,—living upon the coarsest fare that he might bestow his earnings upon "his sick boys,"—of these years he speaks not at all, save as to the causation of his "war paralysis." "Yes, it made an old man of me; but I would like to do it all again if there were need." Of his long years of suffering and his brave and patient confronting of pain, poverty, and imminent death, his "Specimen Days" is the fitting record.

Replying to a question concerning a dainty volume of his poems which lay near us, and which we have been secretly coveting, he says, "You know I have never been the fashion; publishers were afraid of me, and I have sold the books myself, though I always advise people not to buy them, for I fear they are worthless." But when he writes his name and ours upon the title-page, and lays within the cover several por- traits taken at different periods of his life, we wonder if he can ever know how very far from "worthless" the book will be to us. We tender in payment a bank-note of larger denomination than we could be supposed to possess, with a deprecating remark upon the novelty of an author's handling a fifty-dollar note, whereupon he laughs heartily: "A novelty to you, is it? I tell you it's an impossibility to me; why, my whole income from my books during a recent half-year was only twenty-two dollars and six cents: don't forget the six cents," he adds, with a twinkle. Then he assures us that he is not in want, and that his "shanty," as he calls his home, is nearly paid for.

He proposes a walk,—"a hobble" it must be for him,—which may afford opportunity to change the note; and as we saunter toward the river, he leaning heavily upon his cane, it is a pleasure to observe the evident feeling of liking and camaraderie which people have for him.

They go out of their way to meet him and to receive merely a friendly nod, for he stops to speak with none save the children who leave their play to run to him. He seems mightily amused when one wee toddler calls him "Mister Socrates," and he tells us this is the first time he has been so addressed, although he understands that some of his friends speak of him among themselves by the name of that philosopher. So far as he knows, the name was first applied to him in Buchanan's lines "To Socrates in Camden."

Everywhere we go, on the ferry, at the hotel where we lunch, he receives affectionate greeting from people of every rank, yet he is not loquacious, certainly not effusive. He shakes hands but once while we are out, and that is with an unknown man, and because he *is* unknown, as Whitman afterward tells us.

During luncheon we speak of a recent visit to Mrs. Howarth (the poetess "Clementine"). Whitman is at once interested, and questions until he has drawn out the pathetic story of her struggles with poverty, disease, and impeding environment, and then declares he will go to see her as soon as he is able. He declines to receive a copy of her poems, saying he is far more interested in her than he could possibly be in her books, and that he "nowadays religiously abstains from reading poetry." Confirmation of this latter statement occurs in our subsequent conversation. A friend of ours had met Swinburne, and had been assured by that erratic (please don't print it erotic) bard that he thinks Whitman, next to Hugo, the best of recent poets. When we tell our poet of this, and endeavor to ascertain if the admiration be reciprocal, we find him unfamiliar with Swinburne's recent works. Reference to the latter's retraction of his first praise elicits the pertinent observation, "The trouble with Swinburne seems to be he don't know his own mind," but this is followed by warm encomiums upon "Atalanta" and its gifted author.

Whitman had seen Emerson for the last time when the philosopher's memory had failed and all his powers were weakening: instead of being shocked by this condition, Whitman thinks it fit and natural, "nature gradually reclaiming the elements she had lent, work all nobly done, soul and senses preparing for rest." Mentioning George Arnold,—

"Doubly dead because he died so young,"—

we find that Whitman loved and mourned him tenderly. He expresses an especial pleasure

and pride in the successes of the poet Richard
Watson Gilder,—"young Gilder," as he familiarly calls him. He loves Browning, and laments
that "Browning never took to" him. He thinks
our own country is fortunate in having felt the
clean and healthful influences of four such natures
as Emerson, Bryant, Whittier, and Longfellow.

Indeed, he has a good word for everybody,
and discerns laudable qualities in some whom
the world has agreed to contemn and cast out.
He has glowing expressions of affection for his
devoted friends in all lands, and only words of
excuse for his enemies. Of the pharisaic Har-
lan, who dismissed him from a government
clerkship solely because he had, ten years before, published the poems of "Enfans d'Adam,"
he charitably says, "No doubt the man thought
he was doing right." Concerning his harshest
critics, including the author of the choice epithet
"swan of the sewers," he speaks only in justi-
fication: from their stand-point, their denuncia-
tions of him and his book were deserved; "he
never dreamt of blaming them for not seeing as
he sees."

After our return to his "shanty" we read to
him a laudatory notice from the current number
of one of our great magazines, in which one of
his poems is mentioned with especial favor;

whereupon he produces from his trunk a note written some years before from the same magazine, contemptuously refusing to publish that very poem. Evidences like this of a change in popular opinion are not needed to confirm Whitman's faith in his own future, nor in that of the great humanity of which he is the prophet and exponent.

Questioned concerning his habits and methods of literary work, he says he carries some sheets of paper loosely fastened together and pencils upon these "the rough draft of his thought" wherever the thought comes to him. Thus, "Leaves of Grass" was composed on the Brooklyn ferry, on the top of stages amid the roar of Broadway, at the opera, in the fields, on the sea-shore. "Drum Taps" was written amid war scenes, on battle-fields, in camps, at hospital bedsides, in actual contact with the subjects it portrays with such tenderness and power. The poems thus born of spontaneous impulse are finally given to the world in a crisp diction which is the result of much study and thought; every word is well considered,—the work of revision being done "almost anywhere" and without the ordinary aids to literary composition. In late years he wrote mostly upon the broad right arm of his chair.

His Literary Work—Its Aims

Complete equipment for his work was de-
rived from contact with Nature in her abounding moods, from sympathetic intimacy with men
and women in all phases of their lives, and from
life-long study of the best books; these—Job,
Isaiah, Homer, Dante, Shakespeare—have been
his teachers, and possibly his models, although
he has never consciously imitated any of them.
His matter and manner are alike his own; he
has not borrowed Blake's style, as Stedman believed, to recast Emerson's thoughts, as Clarence
Cook alleged. His style would naturally re-
semble that of the Semitic prophets and Gaelic
bards,—" the large utterance of the early gods,"
—because inspired by familiarity with the same
objects: the surging sea, the wind-swept mountain, the star-decked heaven, the forest primeval.

His purpose, the moral elevation of humanity,
he trusts is apparent in every page of his book.
By his book he means " Leaves of Grass," the
real work of his life, representing the truest
thoughts and the highest imaginings of forty
years, to which his other work has been inci-
dental and tributary. After its eight periods of
growth, " hitches," he calls them, he completes
them with the annex, " Good-bye my Fancy,"
and thinks his record for the future is made up;

A Day with the Good Gray Poet

"hit or miss, he will bother himself no more about it."

When questioned concerning the lines whose "naked naturalness" has been an offence to many, he impressively avers that he has pondered them earnestly in these latest days, and is sure he would not alter or recall them if he could.

While not professing a moral regeneration or confessing the need of it, he yet assures us, "No array of words can describe how much I am at peace about God and about death." The author of "Whispers of Heavenly Death" cannot be an irreverent person; the impassioned "prayer"—

"That Thou, O God, my life hast lighted
 With ray of light, ineffable, vouchsafed of Thee.
 For that, O God, be it my latest word, here on my knees,
 Old, poor, and paralyzed, I thank Thee. . . .
 I will cling to Thee, O God, though the waves buffet me.
 Thee, Thee, at least, I know"—

is not the utterance of an irreligious heart. One who has known Whitman long and well testifies that he was always a religious *exalté*, and his stanzas show that his musings on death and immortality are inspired by fullest faith. As we listen to him, calmly discoursing upon the great mysteries,—which to him are now mysteries no longer,—we wonder how many of those who call him "beast" or "atheist" can confront the vast unknown with his lofty trust, to say nothing of actual thanksgiving for death itself!

" Praised be the fathomless universe
   For life and joy, for objects and knowledge curious,
   And for love, sweet love,—but praise ! praise ! praise !
   For the sure-enwinding arms of cool-enfolding death."

We who survive him will not forget his peaceful yielding of himself to "the sure-enwinding arms," nor the abounding trust breathed in his last message, sent back from the mystic frontier of the shadowy realm : " Tell them it makes no difference whether I live or die."

In our chat he discloses a surprising knowledge of men and things, and a more surprising lack of knowledge of his own poetry. More than once it strangely appears that the visitor is more familiar with the lines under discussion than is their author. When this is commented upon he laughingly says, " Oh, yes, my friends often tell me there is a book called ' Leaves of Grass' which I ought to read." So when we, about to take leave, ask him to recite one of his shorter poems, he assures us he does not remem-

ber one of them, but will read anything we
wish. We ask for the wonderful elegy, "Out
of the Cradle endlessly Rocking," and afterward
for the night hymn, "When Lilacs Last in the
Dooryard Bloomed," and his compliance con-
fers a never-to-be-forgotten pleasure. He reads
slowly and without effort, his voice often tremu-
lous with emotion, the lines gaining new grandeur and pathos as they come from his lips.

And this—alas that it must be !—is our final
recollection of one of the world's immortals:
a hoar and reverend bard,—"old, poor, and
paralyzed," yet clinging to the optimistic creeds
of his youth,—throned in his great chair among
his books, with the waning light falling like a
benediction upon his uplifted head, his face and
eyes suffused with the exquisite tenderness of
his theme, and all the air about him vibrating
with the tones of his immortal chant to Death,
—the "dark mother always gliding near with
soft feet."

Another hand-clasp, a prayerful "God keep
you," and we have left him alone in the gathering twilight.

We will not here discuss his literary merits.
The encomiums of Emerson, Thoreau, Bur-
roughs, Sanborn, Stedman, Ruskin, Tennyson,
Rossetti, Buchanan, Sarrazin, etc., show what

he is to men of their intellectual stature; but will he ever reach the great, struggling mass for whose uplifting he wrought? His own brave faith is contagious, and we may discern in the wide-spread sorrow over his death, in the changed attitude of critics and reviewers, as well as in the largely increased demand for his books, evidences of his general acceptance.

His day is coming,—is come. He died with its dawn shining full upon him.

INDEX

Abbot, C. C., 104.

Agassiz, 49, 104, 115.

Alcott, Bronson, 21, 73, 78, 92, 144; Orchard House, 54; Wayside, 58.

Alcott, L. M., 21, 54, 102; Grave, 78; Homes, 21, 55.

Aldrich, 91, 111, 140; In Boston, 92; Ponkapog, 146.

Amesbury, 124.

Auburndale, 146.

Austin, J. G., 102.

Bartlett, G. B., 25, 34, 41.

Bartol, Dr., 48, 94.

Beecher, H. W., 176, 185.

Benson, Carl, 184.

Berkshire, 155–198.

Billings, Josh, 193.

Boston, 83–102.

Bridge, Horatio, 34, 182.

Brook Farm, 147,

Brown, John, 20, 23.

Bryant, W. C., 174, 188, 189, 207.

Burritt, Elihu, 176.

Cambridge, 103.

Carter, Robert, 109.

Channing, W. E., 24, 41, 50, 72, 186; Homes, 22, 24, 52.

Clarke, J. F., 27, 76.

Clough, Arthur, 49, 104, 118.

Concord, 17–80; Battle-Field, 43; River, 39.

Conway, Moncure, quoted, 29, 48.

Cooke, Rose Terry, 193.

Index

Index

Index

Index

THE END.

www.ingramcontent.com/pod-product-compliance
Lightning Source LLC
Chambersburg PA
CBHW030115030726
47498CB00007B/2397